John Harrold.

CONTENTS

STORIES BY IAN ROBINSON
ILLUSTRATED BY JOHN HARROLD
STORY COLOURING BY GINA HART

This book belongs to:

....

....

John Harrold.

RUPERT

THE DAILY EXPRESS ANNUAL

John Harrold

Pedigree
BOOKS

Published by Pedigree Books Limited
The Old Rectory, Matford Lane, Exeter, EX2 4PS.

No 61

£5.99
RU61

One morning, Rupert sets out for
Some shopping from the village store.

One morning, Rupert's mother asks him to go into Nutwood to collect some shopping. "Just a few things we need," she says. "I've made a list so you won't forget . . ." Rupert wonders if any of his friends will be out shopping too. Inside the grocer's he spots Pong-Ping, buying lots of little candles. "Hello!" says Rupert. "Why do you need so many?" "Lanterns!" smiles the Peke. "I'm going to celebrate New Year's Day . . ."

the Dragon Dance

Pong-Ping's there too, but what's he got?
"Small candles! I've just bought the lot!"

"For paper lanterns!" says the Peke.
"It's Chinese New Year's Day next week . . ."

"You're a bit late!" says Rupert. "It's almost the end of January!" "I mean the Chinese New Year!" laughs Pong-Ping. "*It* doesn't begin until next week." Pong-Ping waits until Mr. Chimp has packed Rupert's basket. "Come with me," he says. "I'll tell you all about it . . ." As the chums walk to Pong-Ping's house, he explains how the New Year in China starts with wonderful celebrations where people let off fireworks and hang lanterns in the trees.

"In China there's a great display
Of fireworks to start New Year's Day!"

RUPERT HAS AN IDEA

*"There's feasts and dancing dragons too!
I'll show you what the dancers do . . ."*

*"They dress up as **real** dragons, look!
Just like the pictures in this book . . ."*

*"What fun!" cries Rupert. "This New Year
Let's have a dancing dragon here!"*

*The pair agree. "I'll go and tell
The others. They can dance as well . . ."*

"Everyone in China celebrates New Year's Day!" says Pong-Ping. "As well as all the fireworks there's feasting, music and dancing dragons!" "Dragons!" gasps Rupert. "Yes!" smiles his friend. "Most of them are people dressed up in costumes to look like dragons, but at the Emperor's palace real dragons sometimes come down from the High Mountains to join in too!" Pulling down a book on China, he shows Rupert a picture of the festivities. "It's a marvellous sight," he sighs.

As Rupert gazes at the picture of dancing dragons, he suddenly has a good idea. "Why don't we celebrate in Nutwood?" he asks Pong-Ping. "If we made a dragon costume we could even do a special dance along the High Street . . ." "That would be fun," laughs the Peke. "I'm sure the others will think so too," says Rupert. "I'll tell them all about it while you decide what our dragon should look like." "Excellent," nods Pong-Ping. "We can make a start this afternoon . . ."

RUPERT'S PALS GET READY

"To make a costume's quite a task!"
Says Pong-Ping as he builds a mask.

But finally the dragon's made –
"Just right for our New Year parade!"

"Pong-Ping says it's my job to show
The dragon dancers where to go!"

Old Gaffer Jarge blinks with surprise –
"Young Rupert's dressed up in disguise!"

When Rupert tells his chums about the Dragon Dance, Ottoline and Bill both volunteer to help make the costume. For the next few days the pals gather at Pong-Ping's house, cutting out paper scales for the dragon's body, while the Peke makes an enormous head. At last the costume is finished and Pong-Ping lays it out for everyone to see . . ." "Well done," he smiles. "I'll carry the head, while you two follow inside. Rupert will lead the way with a special lantern."

Next morning, Rupert's mother puts the finishing touches to his costume. "I've got to lead the dragon along the High Street!" he says excitedly. "P.C. Growler has promised to stop the traffic!" "I'm sure it will be splendid!" smiles Mrs. Bear. "We'll all come and watch . . ." As soon as everything is ready, Rupert hurries off towards Pong-Ping's house. On the way he meets Gaffer Jarge, who stares at him in amazement. "Why, 'tis young Rupert," he blinks.

9

RUPERT LEADS THE DRAGON

Pong-Ping likes Rupert's costume too,
"I've got a lantern here for you . . ."

"All set?" calls Pong-Ping. "Follow me!"
The pals set off excitedly . . .

The dragon starts to dance and sway
As Rupert's lantern leads the way.

"A great, green monster!" Gaffer cries,
Unable to believe his eyes!

When Rupert arrives at Pong-Ping's house, he finds the others are almost ready. "Hello!" he calls. "What do you think of my costume?" "Wonderful!" laughs Pong-Ping. "With a lantern to lead us, you'll really look the part." Telling the others to lift up the dragon, he explains they need to hold it above their heads, like an huge umbrella. "Follow me!" he adds. "If we keep in step it will look really convincing. I can't wait to see people's faces when we reach the High Street!"

After a few practice turns around the garden, Pong-Ping declares that they are ready to start and asks Rupert to lead the way. "Left, right! Left, right!" he calls as the great, green monster sets off along the lane . . . On the way they meet Gaffer Jarge, who gazes at the dragon in disbelief. "Happy New Year!" cries Rupert. "Same to you!" blinks Nutwood's oldest inhabitant. "I should have known 'twas another of your pranks! So that's why you're running round in fancy dress . . ."

10

RUPERT'S DRAGON DANCES

In Nutwood everybody cheers
As soon as the dragon appears . . .

"Well done!" calls Pong-Ping. "This is fun!
A Happy New Year, everyone!"

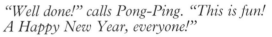

At last the great procession ends.
A crowd congratulates the friends.

Then Nutwood's postman comes to bring
A special letter for Pong-Ping . . .

Leaving Gaffer Jarge behind, the pals keep going until they reach the High Street. Everyone stops in their tracks as the dragon appears, then people start to clap and cheer while Rupert leads it down the middle of the road, past the village stores. "Well done!" Pong-Ping calls to the others. "There can't be a finer dragon in the whole of China! This is a New Year's Day I'll never forget!" "Neither will anyone in Nutwood!" chuckles Bill. "Especially Gaffer Jarge!"

At the end of the dance, Pong-Ping and the others lift the dragon high above their heads and bow to the crowd. "Bravo!" calls Sailor Sam. "I can't believe it looked so lifelike . . ." Before the chums can start back along the High Street, Nutwood's postman calls out to Pong-Ping. "There you are!" he puffs. "I tried calling at your house, but there was no reply. I've got a special letter for you that has come all the way from China. It looks as if it might be something important . . ."

11

RUPERT'S PAL GETS AN INVITATION

*Pong-Ping reads, "Royal Festivities
To mark the New Year – Join us please . . ."*

*"Let's all go!" smiles Pong-Ping. "Then you
Can see **real** dragons dancing too!"*

*"We'll travel in my special lift
The Emperor built as a gift . . ."*

*The pals squeeze in – the lift's quite small,
But Pong-Ping says there's room for all.*

As Pong-Ping starts to read the letter, he turns to Rupert with a cry of delight. "It's an invitation from the Emperor," he explains. "My grandfather used to live at his Court. He's written to ask if I would like to attend the Royal New Year's Celebrations in China!" "That sounds marvellous," says Rupert. "They must be magnificent." "Why don't we all go?" declares Pong-Ping. "I'm sure the Emperor wouldn't mind. We can take our dragon costume and join the other dancers!"

Leading the way to his house, Pong-Ping tells Ottoline about a special lift he owns which will take you all the way to China. "The Emperor had it built as a gift for my father," he explains. "It comes out in the grounds of the Royal Palace . . ." Pong-Ping unlocks the doors of a small, round building and tells the chums to carry the dragon inside. "It's a bit of a crush," says Bill, but eventually they all squeeze in. "I can't wait to see the celebrations!" cries Rupert excitedly.

RUPERT GOES TO CHINA

"Hold tight!" he calls, then off they go –
The next stop's China – miles below . . .

The lift stops. "China! Follow me,
These are the palace grounds you see . . ."

Then Pong-Ping pauses. "Something's wrong!"
There's no sign of the festive throng . . .

An old man sits alone. "Li-Poo!"
Calls Pong-Ping. "Why's no-one with you?"

When everyone is aboard, Pong-Ping presses a button and the lift begins to to move. Down and down it glides, with only a flickering light glimmering overhead. Just as Rupert is wondering how much further they have to go, the lift stops with a jolt and the doors slide open . . . "Welcome to China!" calls Pong-Ping. "Follow me and I will take you to meet the Emperor." "How exciting!" gasps Ottoline as the chums marvel at the beautiful gardens and far-off mountain peaks.

Although the palace looks magnificent, Pong-Ping stops as they approach and gives a cry of surprise. "What's wrong?" asks Rupert. "There's nobody here!" says the Peke. "The courtyard should be hung with lanterns and banners, while everyone gathers to celebrate the Festival." Not a soul stirs as the chums cross the courtyard and the palace seems deserted . . . Suddenly, Pong-Ping spots an old man sitting all by himself. "Li-Poo!" he cries and hurries forward to greet him . . .

13

The Mandarin looks very glum.
"The dancing dragons didn't come!"

"The Emperor's so sad that he's
Abandoned the festivities!"

"Oh, dear!" sighs Pong-Ping. "What a shame!
The New Year just won't seem the same . . ."

"Wait!" Rupert says. "At least let's show
*Them **our** dragon before we go . . ."*

Rupert has often heard Pong-Ping talk of Li-Poo and knows that the old man is one of the Emperor's closest advisors. "Greetings!" he calls as the chums draw near. "You have arrived at a difficult time! Not a single dragon has come to celebrate the New Year . . ." "Really?" blinks Pong-Ping. "I thought they flew down from the High Mountains." "Their absence is a sign of great misfortune!" nods Li-Poo. "The Emperor is so upset he has cancelled the festivities and taken to his bed!"

"What a pity!" sighs Pong-Ping. "If the celebrations have been cancelled, I suppose we may as well go home." "It might be best," agrees Li-Po. "The Emperor has vowed to see no-one until the dragons return!" The disappointed chums set off towards the lift, when Rupert has a good idea . . . "Why don't we perform our dance anyway?" he asks. "We've brought the costume all this way and it seems a shame just to take it back to Nutwood without anybody seeing . . ."

14

Pong-Ping agrees. "A lively dance
Might cheer things up! Let's take a chance!"

Then, strangely, Rupert thinks that he
Can hear a distant melody.

Pong-Ping can hear a tune as well,
But where's it from? The pals can't tell

"This way's right!" Rupert calls. "I'm sure
The music's louder than before!"

The chums agree to Rupert's plan. "A dragon dance will cheer everyone up!" declares Pong-Ping. "If the Emperor sees us from his window, he might even change his mind and allow the celebrations to go ahead!" While the others are getting the dragon ready, Rupert begins to put on his own special costume. To his surprise, he suddenly hears lively music, playing in the distance. "Somebody must be celebrating, after all!" he thinks. "I wonder who it can be?"

Pong-Ping hears the music too and peers out from under the dragon costume to see what's going on . . . "It's coming from over there," says Rupert. "Let's see if we can spot anyone . . ." Hurrying forward, he leads the Nutwood dragon along a winding path towards the distant hills. "It sounds like a piper!" calls Ottoline. "He's playing some sort of jig." "Yes," says Pong-Ping, recognising the tune. "It's a famous dance that real dragons find irresistible . . ."

15

RUPERT SPOTS A PIPER

A piper! And the tune he blows
Is one that Pong-Ping's says he knows . . .

"No dragon can resist this dance –
It makes them follow in a trance . . ."

"He thinks we're real! Let's follow too –
Keep hidden so he can't see you!"

The piper starts to march away,
Convinced the dragon's in his sway . . .

Hurrying towards the sound of the music, Rupert spots a man dressed in long robes, playing a high-pitched pipe. "A stranger!" hisses Pong-Pong. "He's not one of the Emperor's men . . ." As soon as he catches sight of the Nutwood Dragon, the piper starts to move away, beckoning for the chums to follow. "Keep out of sight!" Pong-Ping tells Rupert. "We'll pretend to be a real dragon and find out what he's up to. As long as he keeps playing, we'll dance wherever he leads . . ."

With Rupert at their side, Pong-Ping and the others dance through the palace gardens after the mysterious piper . . . "He must be the reason why no dragons appeared at this year's festival," says the Peke as they stop to get their bearings. "Any who heard him play would be bound to follow . . ." "Perhaps you're right!" agrees Rupert. As they start off again, he sees the piper has left the palace and is marching away towards the distant hills. "I wonder where he's going?" he thinks.

RUPERT FOLLOWS THE PIPER

*The magic flautist pipes and trills
His way towards the distant hills.*

*"A cave mouth!" Rupert gasps. "Now we
Know where the **real** dragons must be!"*

*The chums grow nervous but decide
To follow the piper inside . . .*

*As Rupert leads the pals, he's shocked
To find the way ahead is blocked!*

Pretending to be a real dragon, the Nutwood chums follow the piper towards the far-off hills. As Rupert runs along beside them, he sees the man making for a rocky mound. "What's he up to?" hisses Pong-Ping. "I don't know," says Rupert. "He's still playing the same dance!" As the chums near the base of the rocks, they see where the piper is going . . . "There's a hidden cave!" calls Rupert. "He's disappearing inside!" "Don't stop!" cries Pong-Ping. "We mustn't let him get away . . ."

The cave in the hillside is so dark that no-one can see where it ends. "Do you think we ought to go in?" asks Bill. "It does look a bit gloomy," admits Rupert. "But if the Piper has anything to do with the disappearing dragons we might discover what's happened to them all . . ." The chums finally agree to take a look, with Rupert leading the way as the others follow him along a narrow tunnel cut in the rock. Suddenly, he feels something blocking the way. "We've come to a dead end!"

RUPERT AND HIS PALS ARE CAUGHT

"Turn back!" calls Bill, but it's too late –
Behind them shuts a heavy gate.

"We're moving!" Rupert gives a start.
"This cage must be some sort of cart!"

The tunnel widens. Onward speeds
The piper, whipping up his steeds.

The pals spot light. "It seems our ride
Has gone right through the mountainside!"

Rupert and Bill turn back towards the entrance of the cave, only to see a heavy wooden door clang shut behind them . . . "We're trapped!" gasps Bill. As Rupert's eyes get used to the dark, he realises that they've wandered into a large, wooden cage. "The floor's shaking!" cries Ottoline. "We're moving forward!" Through a small window, Rupert can see that their cage is moving along the narrow tunnel. "We must be on some sort of cart," he murmurs. "The piper's tricked us too!"

Before long, the tunnel begins to grow wider and the chums can feel the wagon gaining speed. Rupert hears the sound of horses' hooves and the crack of a whip as the piper urges them to go faster and faster. "I can see daylight!" he calls to the others. "We must be nearing the end . . ." "But where are we?" asks Ottoline. "The Land Beyond the Far Hills," says Pong-Ping. "I've often heard talk of such a realm, but never dreamed that there was a secret passage through the mountains . . ."

The piper gives his whip a crack
Then races down a mountain track.

"A palace!" Pong-Ping cries. "Now we
Will see whose prize we're meant to be . . ."

The piper laughs. "Home safe and sound!
Just wait till Chang sees what I've found!"

The palace has a private zoo
Of dragons who've been captured too!

The wagon emerges from the tunnel, then speeds along a winding mountain track. "Few people have ever ventured beyond the Far Hills!" says Pong-Ping. "The Emperor forbids us to cross them and their snowy peaks are the haunts of wild beasts . . ." For a long time all the chums can see is thick forest and distant hills. Then Rupert spots a far-off building, with many towers and turrets. "A palace!" blinks Pong-Ping. "The piper must be taking our dragon as a prize for his master!"

When they reach the palace, the wagon speeds through an enormous gateway, then stops in the middle of a courtyard. "Home at last!" laughs the piper. "Just wait till Chang sees what I've brought him . . ." Peering out of a window, Rupert catches sight of a low building by the far wall. "It looks like a prison!" he gasps. At that moment, he catches sight of some dragons, who stare sadly at the wagon. "There are dozens!" whispers Rupert. "They must be in a private zoo . . ."

RUPERT KEEPS OUT OF SIGHT

The piper tells his master how
He's caught another dragon now . . .

Chang sees the dragon, locked inside,
But Rupert manages to hide.

"A beauty!" smiles Chang. "Come and eat.
The dragon's safe. You've earned a treat!"

"Phew!" Rupert gasps. "The courtyard's clear
It's time that we got out of here!"

Peering out of the window, Rupert spots the piper greeting his master, who comes hurrying down a flight of steps, delighted that the wagon has returned . . . "Another dragon from beyond the Hills!" he cries. "I must see it at once!" As Chang looks in at the chums it is clear that their costume has fooled him completely. Rupert stays hidden in the shadows and waits anxiously to see what will happen next. "So long as no-one knows I'm here, I might just manage to give them the slip . . ."

For a moment, Rupert thinks that Chang will want to see the dragon dancing straightaway. To his relief, he turns instead to the piper and invites him into the palace for a meal. "You have done well!" he beams. "We will see how the new dragon dances tomorrow, but for now we can leave it safely in its cage." "Phew!" gasps Pong-Ping. "That was close!" The chums wait for it to grow dark, then begin to plan their escape. "Nobody seems to be about!" declares Rupert. "They must all be inside."

RUPERT PLANS AN ESCAPE

The heavy door lifts gradually
Until the pals can scramble free.

"Quick!" Pong-Ping calls. "Towards the gate!
They'll spot us if we hesitate . . ."

"Chang's other dragons!" Rupert blinks.
"We can't just leave them here!" he thinks.

"There's one more thing we have to do –
Make Chang give up his private zoo!"

"Let's try the door," suggests Ottoline. "It slid shut behind us but I don't think it's locked . . ." Taking a pole from the dragon costume, the pals all push at the door as hard as they can. At first nothing happens, then it slowly starts to move . . . "Keep pushing!" calls Rupert. While Bill and the others hold it open, Rupert quickly jams the door with the wooden pole. "Hurry!" cries Pong-Ping as the chums clamber out. "We've got to get to the main gate before anyone sees . . ."

Setting off across the deserted courtyard, the chums suddenly hear something moving in the darkness . . . "The other dragons!" gasps Ottoline. "I'd forgotten that Chang had trapped them too." "We can't just go off and leave them here," declares Rupert. He thinks hard for a moment, then tells the others he has thought of a plan. "Unlock their cages, but tell them to stay where they are!" he calls. "If everything goes as it should, we'll teach this Emperor a lesson he won't forget!"

RUPERT PLAYS A TRICK

Next morning Chang arrives to see
His latest dragon properly . . .

The cage is opened wide and then
The piper starts to play again.

The Nutwood dragon starts to prance
Then moves off in a lively dance.

The piper stops and gives a cry –
His puzzled master can't see why . . .

Next morning, when Chang comes to inspect the new dragon, everything in the courtyard looks exactly as it did the night before. From his hiding place, Rupert can see the piper and two guards, who hurry forward to open the cage . . . "Splendid!" exclaims the Emperor. "With all these dragons at my court, good fortune will smile on me, just as the legends fortell . . ." The cage door opens and Nutwood's dragon starts forward, swaying to the piper's tune.

As the sound of the pipe grows louder, the new dragon emerges from its cage and begins to dance round the courtyard . . . "Bravo!" cheers Chang. "A most unusual display!" "Just wait," laughs Rupert, peeping out from his hiding place. All of a sudden, the piper stops playing and drops his instrument with a startled cry. "The dragon!" he gasps, taking a step back and cowering in terror . . . "Whatever's wrong?" blinks the Emperor. "Why have you stopped? I thought it danced very well . . ."

22

RUPERT SURPRISES CHANG

Chang turns to find a fearsome beast –
The dragons have all been released!

The piper and his men all flee.
"Come back!" calls Chang. "You can't leave me!"

The magic flute has lost its power –
The dragons stand their ground and glower!

"Spare me!" begs Chang. "I promise to
Stop catching dragons for my zoo!"

"Behind you, Sire!" gasps the piper. Chang spins round, only to see a real dragon, glaring down angrily . . . "The dragons have escaped," calls a soldier. "Run for your lives!" "Stop!" shouts the Emperor as the piper runs off too. "I command you to recapture these beasts immediately!" "Too late," chuckles Rupert. "You wanted your court to be full of dragons and now you've got your wish." "Help!" wails Chang. "I didn't mean any harm. I only wanted to see them dance . . ."

As he speaks, Chang spots the piper's magic flute lying on the ground. Snatching it up with a cry of triumph, he starts to play, commanding all the dragons to dance . . . To his astonished dismay, they pay no attention to the bewitching tune, but close ranks around him in a menacing circle. "I surrender!" he cries, falling to his knees. "If the flute has lost its power, there is no more I can do! Spare me and I promise never to catch another dragon as long as I reign!"

*"Good!" Pong-Ping smiles. "My friends all heard.
We'll make sure that you keep your word!"*

*"Tricked!" Chang gasps, for each dragon's ear
Was blocked up, so it couldn't hear . . .*

*"The magic flute will play no more –
We'll take it with us to make sure!"*

*The dragons want to thank Pong-Ping.
"What can you do? There is one thing . . ."*

Rupert gestures for the dragons to move aside as Pong-Ping peers out from beneath the chums' costume. "No harm will befall you, but be sure to keep your promise!" he cries. Chang stares in astonishment to see that the Nutwood dragon isn't real. "You tricked me!" he gasps. "But why didn't the flute make the other dragons dance?" "They couldn't hear it!" laughs Rupert, pulling a paper scale from the largest creature's ear. "We decided to turn the tables and teach you a lesson!"

"Without the magic flute, you will never command the dragons again!" says Rupert. "From now on they can come and go as they please . . ." As Ottoline and Bill remove the rest of the ear-plugs, the large dragon thanks Pong-Ping for their help. "How can we ever repay you?" it asks. Pong-Ping thinks for a moment then tells it how upset the other Emperor was when no-one came to his New Year celebrations. "We must make amends!" declares the dragon. "Let's all go together . . ."

RUPERT RIDES A FLYING DRAGON

The chums enjoy a dragon ride
Across High Peaks to the far side . . .

They spot a palace down below –
"Hurray! That's where we want to go!"

"Look!" Li-Poo cries. "It's not too late!
Dragons have come to celebrate!"

Then, as the dragons land, he comes
To welcome the returning chums.

Rupert is delighted the dragons have agreed to take part in the New Year celebrations. "Climb on my back!" their leader tells him. "We will carry you and your friends to the far side of the mountains." In no time at all, the chums are soaring over the palace walls and up into the sky. Around them, dragons of all shapes and sizes flap their wings and urge each other on. As they reach the mountains, Rupert can see snowy peaks, shrouded in cloud. "There's the palace!" cries Ottoline . . .

Down in the palace courtyard, the arrival of the dragons causes great excitement. Li-Poo calls delightedly to the Emperor, who peers out of his bedroom window and blinks in astonishment. With a cry of wonder, he hurries to get dressed, then runs out into the courtyard. "Hello!" calls Rupert as the large dragon swoops down. "We've come to join in the celebrations . . ." "Welcome back!" calls Li-Poo. "Where have you been? I searched everywhere, but you'd all disappeared!"

RUPERT JOINS THE CELEBRATIONS

*"So **that** was why no dragons came!
I might have known Chang was to blame!"*

*"I'll lock his magic flute away,
So nobody can make it play!"*

*At last the dancers all begin
And Nutwood's dragon soon joins in . . .*

*The Emperor lets out a cheer,
"Thank you, my friends. Happy New Year!"*

Rupert tells the Emperor how all the dragons had been lured away by Chang. "So that's why none came to my Court," he smiles. "I thought they were displeased and had decided to withhold their greeting." "No," smiles Rupert. "They intended to visit you all the time." Studying the magic flute carefully, the Emperor orders Li-Poo to lock it away, where it can do no harm. "Dragons should be free to come and go as they please!" he declares. "Now they always will be, thanks to you . . ."

Now that all the dragons are safe, the Emperor declares that he will hold a grand New Year's procession to celebrate. Everyone is delighted and the chums decide to join in with their own costume, just as they had originally planned . . . "Well done!" cheers the Emperor as they dance past, together with the real dragons. "This is the best and finest Festival I can remember. Happy New Year everyone! And thank you all for your help!"

THE END

RUPERT
and the
Lost Sheep

John Harrold.

RUPERT HAS A STRANGE AWAKENING

Each evening Rupert likes to look
At pictures in his favourite book.

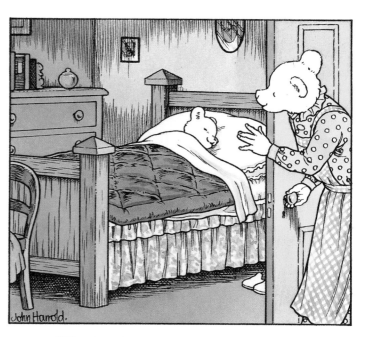

"That's quite enough rhymes for tonight!"
Says Mrs. Bear. "It's late! Sleep tight!"

But that night Rupert dreams that he
Is floating, like a ship at sea . . .

A fish leaps over Rupert's head.
"Be careful – don't fall out of bed!"

One evening, when Rupert is ready for bed, Mrs. Bear agrees to read from one of his favourite books. Gazing at the pictures, he listens delightedly and enters a world where kings are merry old souls, cows eat buttercups and the seas are made of ink. "Just one more!" he pleads, but Mrs. Bear says it is time to stop. "We'll read some more tomorrow," she smiles. "Off to the Land of Nod now, Rupert. Sweet dreams!" Rupert snuggles down and is soon fast asleep . . .

During the night, Rupert wakes with a sudden start. "W . . what's happening?" he blinks. "It feels as though I'm falling!" As he sits up he realises that his bed is swaying back and forth, like a ship at sea. "I must be dreaming!" he gasps, but at that moment a fish leaps out of the water and over Rupert's head. "I *am* at sea!" he marvels. "Of course you are!" cries the fish. "Best place to be if you ask me. We've been following your bed for ages. Knew you'd wake up sooner or later!"

RUPERT DRIFTS TO AN ISLAND

"The water's real! My bed's afloat –
Exactly like a little boat!"

"An island!" Rupert gasps. "But how?
I'm drifting straight towards it now . . ."

The rocky island looks quite bare.
"I don't think anybody's there . . ."

But as he lands Rupert sees more
Beds, grounded on the sandy shore.

Looking around him, Rupert sees that his bed is floating on the water, just like a little boat. The sky above is full of stars and everything glints with silvery moonlight. More fish leap up, following Rupert in a flying shoal. "Not long now!" they call. "Your journey's nearly over . . ." At first, Rupert is mystified, all he can see is water on every side. Then, suddenly, he catches sight of a tiny island. "I'm drifting towards it!" he murmurs, standing up to see . . .

As he floats nearer, Rupert sees that the rocky island is covered in bushes and trees. "It looks deserted!" he thinks, but, when he finally reaches the shore he can see lots of other beds, all grounded on the sand, like rowing boats . . . "Where am I?" he blinks. "Who else is here as well? They must all have drifted ashore . . ." Nobody seems to have seen him arrive and all Rupert can hear is the gentle lapping of waves. Slowly he climbs down and sets off to explore.

RUPERT SPOTS A FLOCK OF SHEEP

"I can't see anyone around!"
Thinks Rupert. Then he hears a sound!

"A flock of sheep! Each has a bell.
A shepherd must be here as well . . ."

The sheep move inland from the sea.
"I do believe they're guiding me!"

Then Rupert spots a sign, "This way!"
And hurries off without delay.

Rupert can't see anyone, but as he crosses the sandy beach he hears a strange tinkling sound. "It's coming from behind those bushes!" he thinks and clambers up the rocky path to take a closer look. To Rupert's surprise, he finds a flock of sheep, grazing peacefully in a grassy clearing. "I wonder where they've come from?" he murmurs. "There doesn't seem to be anyone with them, but they're wearing bells round their necks, so there must be a shepherd somewhere on the island!"

Rupert moves closer to the sheep, but as soon as they notice him they stop grazing and run off, away from the shore. "I'll follow them!" he decides. "Perhaps they'll lead me to the shepherd's hut." On the far side of the clearing Rupert discovers a pathway and a strange sign . . . "Arrivals, this way" he reads. "So *that's* where everyone must have gone! I wonder if they're very far ahead?" Full of curiosity, he sets off along the little path to see where it leads.

RUPERT JOINS THE OTHERS

*A train! It's full of children who
Are dressed in their pyjamas too . . .*

*"Come on now, please! The train can't wait
Much longer or we'll all be late!"*

*"Well done!" a boy calls. "Sit with me.
There's one last seat left here that's free!"*

*The journey starts but no-one knows
How long it takes or where it goes . . .*

Rupert follows the path across the island until he suddenly hears the sound of children, laughing and chattering excitedly. Hurrying forward, he sees them all, sitting in the carriages of a waiting train. "Look lively!" cries a ticket clerk. "You're just in time to join the others . . ." Handing Rupert a ticket, he points to the guard, who has his flag raised, ready to signal the driver. "Come along!" he calls. "There's a spare seat left in the last carriage."

"Thanks!" calls Rupert. Waving his ticket, he hops aboard the train. "Well done!" says a boy. "We thought you'd be left behind!" The train chugs forward and everyone settles down to enjoy the ride. "Look!" says the boy. "There are stars in the sky but the moon is as bright as day!" "Do you know where we are?" asks Rupert. "No," his companion replies. "I went to bed normally, then woke up here, down by the shore!" "Me too!" says a little girl. "It's just like a dream!"

Strange sights greet Rupert all around
But none so odd as where they're bound!

Inside the tunnel bubbles rise
Then disappear before his eyes . . .

The train stops. Rupert hears a shout,
"All change!" then everyone gets out.

The children cross a bridge. Now they
Are joined by stars which light the way . . .

Rupert can hardly believe his eyes as the little train trundles across the island. Brightly-coloured butterflies flutter all around, while up in the treetops winged giraffes sit perched in a huge nest. Nearing the mountain in the middle of the island, Rupert is astonished to see that it looks just like a yawning giant . . . "Sleepy Mountain!" calls the driver as they disappear into a tunnel. Inside, the train speeds through a rocky chamber, where magic bubbles rise from a brimming lake . . .

On the far side of the mountain, the sky is full of stars, which sparkle and shine as the moon beams down. "Land of Nod!" calls the driver. "All change!" The train stops and everyone gets out. Ahead of them lies a narrow bridge, across a rocky gorge. As the children run towards it, a shower of stars falls from the sky . . . Rupert blinks in amazement to see them swoop and spin on every side. "They're leading the way!" he laughs. "We've each got a star to guide us!"

RUPERT FOLLOWS A STAR

Astonished, Rupert stops to stare
Then finds his own star waiting there . . .

"Come on!" it calls. "There's more to see
Across the bridge. Just follow me!"

"Enjoy your visit!" calls the star.
"You'll soon find where the others are . . ."

Rupert sets off then, suddenly,
A rattle hits him, from a tree!

Rupert is so busy marvelling at the sights, that he is the last one to set off across the bridge. "Don't worry!" chirps a star. "All you have to do is follow me!" "W . . where are we?" asks Rupert, amazed to find that the star can talk. "Crossing the River of Memories!" it smiles. "The fishermen you can see are looking for things that have been forgotten . . . All our visitors come this way," adds the star. "There's a new group of children every night . . ."

As soon as they are safely across the bridge, Rupert's star starts to float up into the sky. "Follow the signs!" it calls. "You'll soon catch up with all the others!" Rupert sets off along the path and finds himself walking through a wood, with tall trees. To his surprise, he is sure he can hear a baby crying. "I wonder where it is?" he thinks, "There must be someone pushing a pram . . ." The next moment, a rattle tumbles out of the treetops and lands on Rupert's head!

Rupert and the Lost Sheep

RUPERT FINDS A RATTLE

"Somebody must have dropped it! Who?"
He hears a baby crying too . . .

"A flight of steps inside a tree.
I think I'll take a look and see . . ."

As Rupert climbs the stairs he hears
A song which stops the baby's tears.

He clambers up, amazed to see
He's found a tree-top nursery!

"Ow!" says Rupert, rubbing his head as he picks up the rattle. Looking all round, he still can't see any sign of a baby but the sound of crying is louder than ever . . . "It's coming from the top of that tree!" he gasps as a second baby joins the noisy din. Looking more closely at the tree, Rupert is intrigued to find that it has a doorway cut in its base and a flight of steps leading up inside the hollow trunk . . . "I wonder who's up there?" he thinks. "Perhaps it's where somebody lives?"

Inside the hollow tree-trunk, Rupert follows a winding stairway up through the gloom until he suddenly emerges in a thick canopy of green leaves. To his astonishment, he sees a collection of cribs and cradles, all resting precariously on the tree's upper branches. A nursemaid sits singing lullabies to calm the crying babies, while others slumber peacefully, as a gentle wind rocks their cots. "Hush-a-bye, baby!" murmurs Rupert. "It's just like the song!"

He shows the nurse the rattle then
Explains he's brought it back again.

"How kind!" she smiles. "I often go
To search for rattles down below!"

The nurse asks if he'd like to stay.
"It's restful when the branches sway . . ."

But Rupert hurries off to find
The others. "I've been left behind!"

"Hello, dear!" smiles the nursemaid. "Have you come to visit your little brother or sister?" "No," says Rupert and explains how one of the babies must have thrown a rattle out of its crib. "The little rascal!" laughs the nurse. "They're *always* doing that! I wondered why he was making so much noise. It's very kind of you to bring it back. When they're all awake, I'm up and down those stairs all day long!" Shaking the rattle, she hands it to a baby, who grins up at Rupert delightedly . . .

"Would you like to stay and sing some songs?" asks the nursemaid. "The children like it when visitors join in . . ." The gently-swaying nursery is so restful that Rupert feels quite drowsy. "If I fall asleep, I'll never catch up with the others," he thinks. Clambering down the staircase, he sets off along the path as quickly as he can. "I wonder why everyone was in such a rush?" he murmurs. "I caught the train so hurriedly that nobody told me where we were going!"

RUPERT COMES TO A CASTLE

Then, blinking with surprise, he sees
A castle peeping through the trees.

He hurries to the garden then
Spots all the others, once again.

"Hello!" a boy calls. "Join the fun –
The party's already begun!"

On every side that Rupert looks
Are well-known characters from books!

As he hurries along, Rupert notices colourful lanterns hanging in the trees. "This must be the right direction," he thinks. "They're lighting the way, like a glowing trail . . ." Rounding the corner, he suddenly catches sight of an imposing castle, with turrets and towers which rise high above the trees. Approaching the castle grounds, Rupert hears the sound of voices and spots some children from the train. "I wonder what's happening?" he blinks. "It looks like some sort of party . . ."

Rupert runs to join the others. "Hello!" calls a boy. "We were wondering where you'd got to . . ." "It's a wonderful party!" smiles his friend. "You must be one of the last guests to arrive." All around him, Rupert can see children talking happily with characters he seems to recognise . . . "Algy!" he gasps, astonished to see his chum. At that very moment a footman arrives with a silver tray. "Have some lemonade!" he smiles. "You must be thirsty after coming all that way!"

RUPERT MEETS BO-PEEP

A shepherdess begins to cry.
"She looks upset! I wonder why?"

"Hello!" she sniffs. "I've lost my sheep!"
"Then you must really be Bo-Peep!"

"Perhaps it was your sheep I saw!
A whole flock, grazing by the shore!"

"Come on. Let's go! I'll show you where.
With any luck they'll still be there!"

Rupert takes a glass of lemonade, then turns to join his chums. The garden is so full of guests that he loses sight of Bill and Algy in the crowd . . . "It's like a huge fancy dress ball!" he murmurs. "Everyone looks as if they've come from a Nursery Rhyme!" Just then, Rupert spots a little girl, crying all by herself. "What's wrong?" he asks. "Why are you so sad?" "I've lost my sheep!" sobs the girl. "Sheep?" blinks Rupert. "Then you must be Little Bo-Peep!"

Rupert can hardly believe the girl he has met is really Bo-Peep. "I think I can help you!" he smiles. "I saw a flock of sheep when I first arrived. They were wandering about, down by the shore . . ." "I didn't think of looking there!" cries the girl. "They normally keep to the middle of the island. I fell asleep while they were grazing and when I woke up they'd all gone!" "Come on!" says Rupert. "I'll show you where I saw them. With a bit of luck they'll still be there . . ."

The pair run back to catch the train.
They wake the driver and explain . . .

In no time they are speeding back
Along the winding railway track.

The Clerk and Guard are fast asleep.
"They haven't seen us!" smiles Bo-Peep.

The sheep have disappeared. "Oh, dear!
I'm certain that I left them here . . ."

Hurrying off in search of the missing sheep, Rupert and Bo-Peep run along the path, towards the little train. The driver looks surprised to see them but agrees to make a special journey. "I hope the sheep haven't gone far!" says Bo-Peep. "I need to get them rounded up again straightaway . . ." As they trundle through the tunnel to the far side of Sleepy Mountain, Rupert wonders why Bo-Peep is in such a rush. "They have to be at the palace before the party ends!" she frets.

When the train reaches the end of the line, Rupert and Bo-Peep find the ticket clerk is sound asleep . . . "We'll try not to wake him," whispers Rupert. "There can't be any trains due till the end of the party!" Setting off along the path, he leads Bo-Peep to the spot where he last saw the sheep. "They must have wandered off!" he sighs. "I thought they'd still be here." "They can't have gone far," says Bo-Peep. "Please help me find them! I need to get the whole flock back to the palace . . ."

RUPERT FINDS BOY BLUE

Then Rupert spots a trail. "Come on!
We'll follow it to where they've gone!"

"My sheep!" cries Bo-Peep happily.
"But those are Boy Blue's cows I see . . ."

The cowherd's sleeping, like the rhyme –
"I think we've found him just in time!"

"Wake up!" calls Bo-Peep. "Blow your horn.
Your cows are trampling down the corn!"

As he searches for the missing sheep, Rupert suddenly spots a trail of trampled grass . . ."Come on!" he cries. "They must have gone this way!" Across the fields, the pair hear the distant tinkle of bells and soon spot the whole flock, grazing in a meadow. "Hurrah!" cries Bo-Peep. To Rupert's surprise, the next field is full of grazing animals too. "A herd of cows!" he gasps. "They shouldn't be there! They'll break down all the corn." "Oh, dear!" says Bo-Peep. "We'll have to find Boy Blue!"

"Boy Blue?" murmurs Rupert. "Of course! Sheep in the meadow and cows in the corn . . ." "And not a sign of him anywhere!" sighs Bo-Peep. "Perhaps if we look behind the haystacks?" suggests Rupert. "Let's go and see!" Sure enough, they soon find the cowherd, lying fast asleep . . . "Wake up!" calls Bo-Peep. "There's a terrible muddle and we need your help to sort things out!" "What's that?" yawns the boy. "I was only having forty winks. Goodness! Whatever's been happening?"

RUPERT DISCOVERS A SHORT CUT

"I'll help you!" Rupert tells Bo-Peep
As she sets out to herd the sheep.

The sheep seem overjoyed and all
Come running when they hear her call.

Boy Blue says that he knows how they
Can reach the palace straightaway . . .

"Keep going and you'll soon be there.
It won't take long!" he tells the pair.

"No time to explain!" calls Bo-Peep. "Rupert and I will start rounding up sheep, while *you* herd all the cows . . ." To Rupert's surprise, the sheep seem overjoyed to see their mistress and trot obediently behind one another wherever she leads. Boy Blue takes his horn and signals to the wandering cattle. Long, clear notes ring out across the fields and the cows turn back as well. "Thank goodness we caught them!" says Bo-Peep. "Any later and they'd have been scattered everywhere . . ."

When the last cow has been cleared from the corn and the sheep are gathered in a flock, Bo-Peep finally tells Boy Blue what has happened and how she needs to get back to the palace right away . . . "The palace?" he smiles. "That's easy! There's a special short cut which will get you there much faster than railways and bridges. One of my cows found it, the last time they wandered off . . ." Leading the way to a narrow gorge, he points to a steep pathway cut in the rock.

RUPERT RETURNS TO THE CASTLE

The sheep set off in single file
Across the middle of the isle.

Bo-Peep explains she has to bring
Her flock each night to see the King.

"But why?" asks Rupert. "Everyone
Is in the garden, having fun . . ."

"Don't fret!" Bo-Peep smiles. "You'll soon see
The reason the King's sent for me . . ."

Driving the sheep forward, Rupert and Bo-Peep set off along the pathway, with the sides of the gorge towering overhead. "Fancy nobody knowing this way!" laughs Bo-Peep. "It must have been made when the palace was built . . ." Rupert still can't think why Bo-Peep needs to reach the palace so urgently. "Do you often take your sheep there?" he asks. "Oh, yes!" replies the shepherdess. "The King insists they appear each evening. It's one of the island laws . . ."

As they near the palace, Rupert can hear that the party is in full swing. He is still amazed the King should have sent for a flock of sheep . . . "Won't they get in the way?" he asks. "The garden's nearly full!" "Don't worry!" smiles Bo-Peep. "Everyone will be expecting them. They signal the end of the party. It's another of our rules." "What happens then?" asks Rupert. "Wait and see!" laughs Bo-Peep. "You'll soon understand why I was so worried about being late . . ."

The party guests all gather round,
Delighted that the sheep are found.

"This way!" a footman calls. "Come in,
The King is ready to begin . . ."

The King sits up. "Hello, Bo-Peep.
Come in, my dear, and bring your sheep!"

Then Rupert laughs and shakes his head
As each one leaps across the bed.

Following the sheep into the garden, Rupert finds all the characters he met earlier are gathered round expectantly. "Here they are!" calls Humpty Dumpty. "I *knew* Bo-Peep would find them . . ." "Well done!" calls another voice. "You're just in time!" "In time for what?" wonders Rupert. "This way," says Bo-Peep and hurries towards the Royal Apartments, where a footman stands waiting. Beckoning to the sheep, he ushers them towards a regal figure who sits propped up in bed . . .

"Come in, come in!" calls the King. "Delighted to see you, my dear. I was beginning to think you must have got lost . . ." Bo-Peep explains what happened and how Rupert helped her round up the missing sheep. "Splendid!" smiles the King. "If you're ready now I think I'll start counting. It's time the party ended and everyone went to sleep . . ." To Rupert's astonishment, the sheep begin to jump over the foot of the bed as the King slowly counts them, one by one . . .

RUPERT FALLS ASLEEP

"You're counting them!" he laughs. "I see!
The same thing always works for me."

Then Rupert starts to count the sheep.
He yawns and soon falls fast asleep!

He wakes up, back in bed again.
"I must have just been dreaming then!"

But then he gasps, amazed to find
A ticket that's been left behind."

"Counting sheep!" laughs Rupert. "That's what my mother always tells *me* to do when I can't get to sleep . . ." "Never fails!" nods the King as Bo-Peep's flock springs over his bed. "Thirty-four, thirty-five, thirty-six . . ." As Rupert watches, he starts to count the sheep too. "I didn't think there were this many!" he murmurs drowsily. At last the King shuts his eyes and starts to snore loudly. Rupert feels weary too. He stops counting and is soon fast asleep . . .

When he wakes up, Rupert finds himself back in Nutwood, with sunshine streaming through the window . . . "Bo-Peep! The King! The party!" he blinks. "It must all have been a dream!" Sitting up, he suddenly feels something tucked in his pyjama pocket. "A railway ticket!" he gasps. "Then I *did* go to the Land of Nod, after all!" Putting the ticket safely away, he jumps up and hurries off to tell his parents all about it . . .

RUPERT

The Bears have come on holiday
Along with Bill, to Rocky Bay.

The school holidays have just started. Rupert and his parents have come to Rocky Bay, together with Bill Badger. "Here we are!" says Mrs. Bear as the train arrives. "I can't wait to see the sea again!" As Mr. Bear leads the way from the station, Rupert catches sight of a poster, with a picture of a pirate . . . "It's a fancy-dress competition!" smiles his mother. "Perhaps *we* could enter!" says Rupert. "There's a prize for the best costume!"

and the Pirates

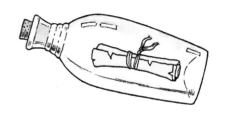

"A Pirate Pageant!" Rupert cries.
"Let's see if we can win the prize!"

Next morning, both the pals prepare
The costumes that they plan to wear . . .

The two chums are so keen to enter the competition that Rupert's parents agree to help them make pirate costumes as soon as they've finished breakfast the next day . . . "There!" says Mr. Bear. "Wooden swords and special hats! You look like a pair of desperadoes, bound for the Spanish Main . . ." With a whoop of delight, the pals go running outside. "Let's go and play on the beach!" Rupert calls to Bill. "First one there can be Captain!"

"Come on!" calls Rupert. "You and me
Can play at pirates by the sea!"

RUPERT PLAYS AT PIRATES

They fight with wooden swords until
Stopped by a sudden cry from Bill . . .

He's spotted something in the sea.
"It's floating, but what can it be?"

"A bottle!" Rupert cries. "I'll try
To catch it while it's bobbing by!"

"Success! And there's a note inside.
It must have drifted on the tide . . ."

Down at the water's edge, Rupert and Bill have great fun, playing at pirates. Scrambling over the rocks, the pair battle furiously, until Bill stops suddenly and points out to sea . . . "There's something floating in the water!" he cries. Rupert looks out across the waves to where Bill points. "It's a bottle!" he cries excitedly. "Perhaps there's something in it? There might be a message!" The two chums hurry out across the rocks to see if they can reach their prize.

Rupert and Bill wait anxiously as the bottle slowly drifts nearer and nearer. "There's a cork in the top!" calls Rupert. Reaching out as far as he can, he grabs the bottle before it floats past and holds it up for Bill to see. "There is something inside!" gasps his pal. "It looks like a note . . ." "I wonder who can have sent it?" says Rupert. "In stories, it's always castaways on desert islands!" "It looks as if it must have come a long way!" murmurs Bill. "Let's take the cork out and see . . ."

RUPERT FINDS A MAP

"The note says, 'Help! A mutiny!'
I wonder where the ship can be?"

"A map!" blinks Bill. "There's Rocky Bay,
And Silversand, not far away . . ."

"I wonder if it's real?" "Let's show
Old Cap'n Binnacle. He'll know!"

The Cap'n spots the pair. "You two
Look like you've joined a pirate crew!"

At first the cork in the bottle seems stuck fast, but at last the two chums manage to prise it out. "What does it say?" asks Bill as Rupert reads the note. "Mutiny aboard the *Gold Doubloon!*" gasps Rupert. "It's somebody asking for help . . ." Turning the note over, the pair are astonished to find a map of Rocky Bay, with a large cross marked near the next headland. "Silversand!" blinks Rupert. "That's not far at all, but what can it all mean?

Puzzled by their find, the two chums don't know what to make of the mysterious note . . . "It sounds like a pirate ship," says Bill, "but there can't be any of those near here!" "I wonder?" says Rupert, then catches sight of Cap'n Binnacle's cabin. "Let's go and ask the Cap'n," he suggests. "He knows about *everything* in Rocky Bay . . ." When the chums reach the cabin, they find their old friend sitting outside, mending his nets. "Hello, lads!" he laughs. "Playing at pirates today?"

RUPERT VISITS CAP'N BINNACLE

Then Rupert shows his friend the note.
"I think it might be from a boat . . ."

"A map! I know the spot it shows –
A bay where no-one ever goes . . ."

"It's not an easy place to reach.
There's just one pathway to the beach."

"When pirates sailed near here they'd land
To share their spoils at Silversand!"

When Cap'n Binnacle hears how Rupert and Bill have found a message in a bottle, he pulls out his spectacles and peers thoughtfully at the note. "Bless me!" he blinks. "It sounds as though somebody's in trouble . . ." "There's a map on the other side!" says Rupert. "I think it's the next bay along the coast." "Silversand!" nods the Cap'n. "'Tis the next bay, to be sure, but mighty difficult for folks to reach. We used to go there when I was a lad, through a gap in the rocks . . ."

"Silversand has always been hard to reach," says Cap'n Binnacle. "In olden days, 'twas a favourite hideaway for smugglers. They'd come ashore and divide their spoils before the Excise men could reach 'em. Many's the time the skull and crossbones was spotted from Rocky Bay – with pirates like Cap'n Morgan, Blind Pew and William Kidd all landing at Silversand with chests full of booty! My old pa used to tell me about 'em in the winter evenings . . ."

RUPERT SHOWS HIS PARENTS

"The only laws that they obeyed
Were ones that old King Neptune made!"

"But that was long ago! Now we
Just don't have mutinies at sea!"

"The Cap'n's right, but I still feel
The note we found just might be real . . ."

"It looks quite real!" says Mr. Bear.
"But then they'd be a ship somewhere!"

"Lawless times!" chuckles Cap'n Binnacle as he recalls Silversand's pirates. "The only power they feared was King Neptune's!" he says, pointing to a carved figure-head. "All sailors obey him, pirates and Navy men alike . . ." Looking through a list of ships, the Cap'n finds no sign of the *Gold Doubloon* and tells Rupert he thinks the note is probably some sort of joke. "Mutinies don't happen much nowadays," he laughs, "and there hasn't been a ship moored off Silversand for years."

As the pair hurry back to Rocky Bay for tea, they agree to visit Silversand as soon as they can. "It will be quite a clamber to reach the beach," says Rupert, "but I'm sure we can do it if we take care . . ." Rupert's parents don't know what to make of his discovery. "It *looks* real enough," says Mr. Bear, "but if Cap'n Binnacle's never heard of the ship then perhaps it's only a hoax." "Plenty of time to find out tomorrow!" smiles Mrs. Bear. "Come and have some tea . . ."

RUPERT AND BILL GO EXPLORING

Next day the chums decide that they
Will try to find the hidden bay.

"This must be where it starts but how?
We can't go any further now . . ."

Then Rupert finds a path between
The rocks, down to the beach they've seen.

"There's no-one here but you and me –
No sign of any mutiny!"

Next morning, Rupert and Bill set off towards the beach as soon as they have finished breakfast. They can see the rocky headland where Silversand Bay begins but, to their disappointment, it seems to be completely cut off by the tide . . . "Let's climb out over the rocks and have a closer look," says Bill. "There might be a path we can take!" The pair clamber carefully from rock to rock but can only peer down at the deserted beach, which seems impossible to reach . . .

Just as the chums are about to give up, Rupert spots a narrow gap in the rocks. "That must be the way Cap'n Binnacle told us about!" says Rupert. "Let's try it and see . . ." Squeezing through the hole in the rocks, the pals find a narrow path that leads down to the beach. "No wonder Silversand was a pirate haunt!" says Rupert. "Ships could have landed here secretly and unloaded chests full of treasure without being noticed by anyone in Rocky Bay . . ."

RUPERT'S PAL FINDS A CAVE

Bill spots a footprint. "Someone's here!
The trail they've left seems pretty clear . . ."

"A cave!" he gasps. "Perhaps we'll find
A treasure chest's been left behind?"

"Gosh!" Rupert blinks. "I'd no idea
There were so many tunnels here!"

Then, suddenly, they see a light.
"Quick, hide!" calls Bill. "Keep out of sight!"

"No pirates here nowadays!" says Bill, then he suddenly notices a trail of footprints in the sand. "They must be recent!" says Rupert. "Otherwise they'd have been washed away by the tide . . ." Following the trail along the shore, the chums are astonished to come to a cave in the cliffs. "Do you think it's a hideout?" whispers Bill. The pair tiptoe forward towards the mouth of the cave. "Perhaps it's got something to do with the note we found about the *Gold Doubloon*!" says Rupert.

Peering into the cave, Rupert and Bill find a rocky tunnel which twists and turns away from the shore. "It must be where the old pirates used to hide their treasure!" says Bill. "Perhaps the *Gold Doubloon* was one of their ships and the note was to throw us off the trail . . ." Before the pair have gone much further, they suddenly hear a murmur of voices and see a glimmer of light advancing towards them. "Hide!" calls Bill. "There's somebody coming . . ."

RUPERT SPOTS REAL PIRATES

*The two men who appear are dressed
As pirates. "Look! They've got a chest!"*

*"Well done, Jed!" says the first. "We've got
His treasure. Now we'll keep the lot!"*

*The pals keep watching while the men
Decide to hide the chest again.*

*Bill trips. A pirate calls, "Who's there?"
Then shines his lantern at the pair.*

Ducking down out of sight, the chums see two men emerging from the gloom . . . "Pirates!" gasps Rupert. "They're carrying a treasure chest too!" From their hiding place, the pals hear the pirates, talking about their haul. "Well done, Jed!" says the first man. "We finally found old Cutlass' gold! Been searching so long, I'd given up hope!" "Aye!" nods the second pirate. "But it's all ours now! We'll leave it here till darkness falls, then row it out to the ship . . ."

To the pals' alarm, they realise that the pirates plan to leave their treasure near the same rock that they're hiding behind. Hardly daring to breathe, they tiptoe away towards the gloom of cave, where the pirates won't see them . . . Just as it seems that all is well, Bill trips on a stone and goes sprawling, head over heels. "What's that?" cries one of the pirates. "There's somebody here! Look, Jethro! 'Tis a couple of snooping landlubbers . . ." "Bless me!" calls the second man. "You're right!"

RUPERT AND BILL ARE CAUGHT

The pirates catch the chums. "Quick, Jed!
These two heard everything we said!"

"Now you know where our treasure's stored
We'll have to keep you safe on board!"

The pirates say when darkness comes
They'll fetch their gold and free the chums . . .

Their ship is moored well out of sight.
"She'll stay there till we sail tonight!"

"Catch 'em!" calls the first pirate, seizing hold of Rupert. "Can't have these two telling the Excise men everything they've seen!" "Right you are!" nods his companion. "We'll have to take them with us . . ." "'Tis only till nightfall," the pirate tells Rupert as he carries him out of the cave. "When we're clear of Silversand, you can tell your tale to anyone who'll listen." "W . . where are you taking us?" asks Bill. "There can't be a ship. We've searched the whole bay!"

Striding to the far end of the bay, the pirates lift Rupert and Bill into a rowing boat that is hidden by the rocks. "Sit still and ye'll come to no harm!" growls Jed. "That's right!" says Jethro. "We've got no quarrel with you. Only come to collect what's ours . . ." Pulling on the oars, he rows steadily out to sea until they clear the rocky headland and glimpse the open sea beyond. Rupert and Bill blink in amazement, for there lies a pirate galleon, with the Jolly Roger flying from her mast!

RUPERT SEES THE GOLD DOUBLOON

*"Look!" whispers Bill. "The **Gold Doubloon!**"*
"Climb up!" calls Jed. "You'll see her soon . . ."

The crew all glare suspiciously.
Who can these two newcomers be?

The pirate chief scowls as he's told
How Rupert heard about the gold.

"Who knows what else the young pups know?
We'll lock 'em in the brig below!"

"It must be the *Gold Doubloon!*" whispers Bill. "Aye!" says Jethro. "That's the name of the ship. You'll meet the rest of her crew soon enough . . ." He gives a shrill whistle as they arrive and a rope ladder comes tumbling over the side. "Climb up slowly!" the pirate orders. "No tricks, mind, or it'll be the worse for you!" Doing as he is told, Rupert clambers aboard, to find a circle of motley figures lying in wait. "Crikey!" gasps Bill. "They don't look very pleased to see us!"

The pirates stare suspiciously at Rupert and Bill as Jethro explains why he and Jed have had to bring them aboard . . . "Silversand is no place for young pups to go prowling!" declares the chief pirate. "Lock 'em in the brig till we're ready to sail. That way we know they won't blab . . ." Opening a hatch in the deck, Jethro leads the way down a steep flight of steps. "Watch your footing!" he warns. "'Tis dark down here. Any trouble and we might forget to let you out!

The chums are locked inside a room
So dark they can't see through the gloom . . .

Then, suddenly, an angry shout
Calls, "Who's there this time? Let me out!"

A stranger sits up. "Pardon me!
Mistook you both for crew, you see!"

"I'm Captain Cutlass, privateer!
My men have locked me up down here!"

At the bottom of the stairs, the pirate unlocks a heavy door which opens with a loud creak. "T'aint much used!" he says. "In you go, till you hear me come back . . ." As the door slams shut, the chums are plunged into total darkness. "I don't like the look of this!" gasps Bill. "Scurvy knaves!" cries a voice. Spinning round, the chums spot a shadowy figure, stirring in the gloom. "Mutinous rabble!" growls the stranger crossly. "First you lock me in, then you come waking me up!"

As the pals cower together, they spot a finely-dressed figure with a splendid hat. "'Pon my soul!" blinks the stranger. "Fellow prisoners! I thought you were part of the crew! Sorry if I frightened you. The name's Cutlass, Captain of the *Gold Doubloon*! At least, I *was* captain until those knaves seized control of the ship! Nothing but trouble ever since we found the treasure," he sighs. "I promised them a fair share, but that wasn't enough! Shanghaied in my own stateroom . . ."

RUPERT PLANS TO ESCAPE

"A mutiny!" cries Bill. "I knew
The note and map we found were true!"

"Aye!" Cutlass nods. "I searched for years
Then lost my prize to mutineers!"

"Perhaps not!" Rupert says. "We might
Still stop them setting sail tonight!"

"Escape?" blinks Cutlass. "You could try
That hatch, although it's rather high . . ."

"So it was *your* message we found, floating in a bottle!" says Bill, producing the folded map from his pocket. "Yes," says Captain Cutlass. "I managed to throw it overboard before the rascals locked me up. The map belonged to my great-grandfather, Horatio Cutlass. It's *his* treasure that's hidden at Silversand. Nobody believed me when I said it was still there, but I finally convinced the crew to search the caves until we found it . . ."

"Now you've been caught, nobody can save the treasure!" sighs Captain Cutlass. "Unless we raise the alarm!" says Rupert. "If I could get ashore, the coastguard might agree to stop the *Gold Doubloon* from setting sail." "Escape?" blinks the Captain. "There *is* a way out, if you've a head for heights and are small enough to squeeze through that hatch! The crew might not spot you if you wait until it's dark. They'll probably spend all day celebrating then fall asleep on deck . . ."

RUPERT CLIMBS OUT

They wait till dark, when all is still,
Then Rupert lifts the heavy grille . . .

"What luck! The crew won't notice me –
They're all as sleepy as can be!"

So Rupert slowly tiptoes past
A group of pirates near the mast . . .

He searches for a rowing boat
Then spots a barrel – will it float?

As soon as darkness falls, Rupert climbs on to Captain Cutlass's shoulders and reaches up for the grille that covers the hatch. "Push!" urges the Captain. "It won't be locked . . ." Sure enough, the cover swings open and Rupert peers out, into the gloom. Nearby, he can see a burly pirate lying on the deck, with others sleeping all around. "The coast's clear!" he whispers. "Good luck!" calls the Captain as Rupert hauls himself up through the trapdoor and on to the deck . . .

All Rupert can hear as he tiptoes away from the brig is the sound of pirates snoring . . . "No wonder Captain Cutlass told me to wait till the evening!" he murmurs. "They look as if they'll sleep all night!" Even so, Rupert is careful not to make a sound as he looks for ways to escape. By the side of the ship, he spots an empty barrel which suddenly gives him a good idea. "I wonder if it's very heavy?" he thinks. "If I put the bung back, I'm sure it will float . . ."

RUPERT PADDLES ASHORE

When Rupert lets the barrel fall
The pirates hardly stir at all . . .

"This pole should help me row ashore.
I'll use it as a makeshift oar!"

"It's lucky no-one noticed me!"
Thinks Rupert, paddling carefully.

At last he hears a crunching sound
And finds the barrel's run aground.

Heaving the barrel over the side of the ship, Rupert drops it in the water with a loud splash. He turns round to see if the pirates have heard, but they are still sound asleep . . ."I'll need a paddle of some sort too," he thinks, and reaches for a ramrod from one of the nearby cannons. Luckily, the rope ladder the pirates used to climb aboard is still in place and by clambering down carefully Rupert can reach the barrel with the long pole. "Now for the tricky part!" he thinks . . .

To Rupert's relief, the barrel makes an ideal raft, floating in the water like a giant cork. Using the ramrod as a paddle, he glides away from the *Gold Doubloon* without anyone noticing and is soon striking out across the bay . . . "Thank goodness it's a calm night!" he thinks. "If the sea was choppy I'd never reach the shore!" At last Rupert hears a welcome scrunching noise as the barrel runs aground. "Silversand!" he cries. Wading ashore, he hurries off along the beach . . .

*Then Rupert takes the passageway
From Silversand to Rocky Bay . . .*

*"Help! Cap'n Binnacle!" he cries.
His old friend blinks in shocked surprise!*

*"The note we found was true! You see
There really was a mutiny!"*

*"We've got to rescue Bill before
The pirates find you've gone ashore . . ."*

Clambering over the rocks at the far end of the beach, Rupert finds the narrow passage that leads to Rocky Bay. Plunging into inky darkness, he gropes his way along until he emerges on the far side and can see stars twinkling overhead. The only light Rupert can see is from Cap'n Binnacle's cabin, where the windows give a cosy glow. "Just who I need!" he thinks and runs towards it, calling for help. "Who's there?" blinks the Captain. "Young Rupert! Whatever's the matter?"

At first, Cap'n Binnacle thinks Rupert's tale of pirates is some sort of prank, but when he hears about Captain Cutlass, he shakes his head and frowns. "A serious business, mutiny!" he tuts. "And young Bill locked in the brig, you say! Sounds like those ruffians mean to cut and run with the tide! Once the *Gold Doubloon* sets sail the Coastguard will have a hard job to catch her. Best thing would be to take 'em by surprise, but first we'll have to rescue Bill . . ."

RUPERT HAS A SUDDEN IDEA

*"Wait!" Rupert calls. "There's something here
That's given me a good idea . . ."*

*"I need King Neptune's trident for
My plan – and nets! A couple more . . ."*

*The Cap'n's boat's tied up below.
"Come on! You tell me where to go . . ."*

*The pair row out to sea till they
Can see the ship across the bay.*

Cap'n Binnacle says he will alert the
Coastguard straightaway. "Leastways, I can *try*!"
he shrugs. "Wait!" says Rupert "I think you and I
might be able to rescue Bill by ourselves. That
figure-head of King Neptune has given me an
idea . . ." To Cap'n Binnacle's surprise, Rupert
asks him to lift down the carved figure's golden
trident. "We'll need some fishing nets as well,"
says Rupert. "Nets?" blinks the old man. "I've got
plenty of those, but what are you up to?"

Rupert tells Cap'n Binnacle he plans to give the
pirates a surprise. "If we hurry, they should still
be fast asleep," he says. "This way!" cries Cap'n
Binnacle. "There's a flight of steps down to the
beach. You can tell me the rest of your plan as we
row out across the bay . . ." Rounding the rocky
headland, the pair soon spot the *Gold Doubloon*,
and row stealthily towards the silent ship. "Bless
me!" murmurs Cap'n Binnacle. "'Tis a proper
pirate galleon!"

RUPERT WAKES THE PIRATES

"The pirates haven't stirred at all!
Wait here until I give the call!"

Then Rupert clambers up to check
The crew are still asleep on deck . . .

He climbs aboard, but this time makes
So much noise every pirate wakes!

"Stop!" calls an old salt angrily
But Rupert laughs. "You can't catch me!"

By the time they reach the *Gold Doubloon*, Rupert has told Cap'n Binnacle exactly what he plans to do . . . "Wait here until I give the signal!" he whispers, climbing back up the ladder. "Aye, aye!" smiles the Captain. "I'll be ready, have no fear!" Peering over the side of the ship, Rupert sees that the pirates are all sound asleep, exactly as he left them. "Good!" he murmurs, "Let's hope they stay that way till everything's ready!" Clambering aboard, he tiptoes past the slumbering crew . . .

Rupert counts slowly to one hundred, then kicks a wooden bucket across the deck with a mighty clatter . . . The pirates wake suddenly and jump to their feet with cries of alarm. "One of the prisoners!" calls their leader. "Catch him, men!" "Too slow!" laughs Rupert as the pirates chase him round and round the mast. "Hold still!" complains an old salt. "You're making me dizzy!" "We'll soon stop him!" cries another pirate. "There's nowhere to go, except over the side!"

At last the pirates seem to win.
"Help!" Rupert calls. "I won't give in!"

"There's no-one here!" a pirate jeers,
Then gasps as somebody appears . . .

"King Neptune!" wail the frightened crew.
"Aye!" growls the King. "I'm cross with you . . ."

"All prisoners belong to me –
For I'm the one who rules the sea!"

Although Rupert leads them a merry dance, the pirates finally corner him. "Over the side's where you'll go!" snarls their leader. "You're lucky we've treasure to fetch or you'd walk the plank right now!" "Help!" calls Rupert as loud as he can. "There's nobody here . . ." laughs the pirate then breaks off with a startled cry. "King Neptune!" he gasps as the other pirates fall back in alarm. "'Tis the Master of the Depths!" quails one of the crew. "He looks a mite displeased . . ."

"Enough!" booms King Neptune. "'Tis time you seadogs came to heel! Mutiny on the High Seas, pirate against pirate and all for the lure of gold! I'll not abide it any longer! Release the prisoners straightaway!" Quaking with fear, the pirates hurry to obey King Neptune's orders, bringing Bill and Captain Cutlass up from the brig as quickly as they can. "'Pon my soul!" splutters Cutlass as Bill runs forward to join Rupert. "King Neptune, here on *my* ship!"

RUPERT'S TRICK WORKS

The pirates let their captives go
To join King Neptune, down below . . .

"We're free!" laughs Cutlass, happily.
"Who told you of the mutiny?"

"That's Rupert's work!" the King replies.
"It's him that thought of this disguise!"

The friends row back across the bay.
"Let's take the treasure on the way . . ."

With the pirates still cowering in terror, Rupert tells Captain Cutlass to climb down the ladder, where Cap'n Binnacle's boat lies waiting. As soon as everyone is safely aboard, they row quickly away from the *Gold Doubloon*, back towards the shore. "Astounding!" marvels Cutlass. "Rescued from those rapscallions without a shot being fired! But how did you know about the mutiny?" "King Neptune knows all that happens at sea!" comes the stern reply. "Above the waves or down below . . ."

As Neptune finishes speaking, Rupert can't help laughing out loud. "Well done!" he chuckles. "You fooled them all!" "The look on those pirates' faces!" laughs Cap'n Binnacle, removing his disguise. "Scared as a bunch of landlubbers caught in a squall!" "Playacting!" blinks Cutlass. "You took me in as well . . ." Nearing the coast, the pals pass Silversand Bay, where the pirates' treasure lies hidden. "Let's go ashore," says Rupert. "I'm sure I can find the chest!"

RUPERT TAKES THE TREASURE

While Bill keeps watch, the others say
They'll fetch the treasure straightaway.

"At last!" cries Cutlass. "Pirate gold!
Just as the map I found foretold!"

"The pirates know the gold's here too!"
Says Binnacle. "Here's what we'll do . . ."

They empty out the chest and then
All fill it up with rocks again!

Pulling the rowing boat ashore, the two captains follow Rupert to the pirates' cave, while Bill keeps a careful lookout. The ancient chest is exactly where Jed and Jethro left and it, hidden behind a rock. To Rupert's delight, the rusted locks are easy to prise open . . . "At last!" cries Captain Cutlass. "My ancestor's booty from the Spanish Main. I always knew we'd find it!" "Worth a King's ransom!" marvels Cap'n Binnacle. "But what shall we do with it now?"

"We can worry about the treasure later!" says Rupert. "First, we have to stop it falling into the hands of the crew . . ." "Quite right!" nods Cutlass. "I'd rather the Excise men got it than those scurvy knaves!" The two men carry the chest down to the shore and empty it out into Cap'n Binnacle's boat. "Now fill it with rocks!" urges Rupert. "We'll close up the lid and put it back in the cave where we found it." "Hurry!" says Bill. "They'll be coming to fetch it soon . . ."

RUPERT REACHES ROCKY BAY

"We'll put it back exactly where
The pirates left it hidden – there!"

"Come on!" calls Bill. "I heard a shout.
The pirates' boat has just set out!"

The chums race back, around the shore
Until they're out of sight once more . . .

"Phew!" Cutlass gasps. "I really thought
They spot us and we'd all be caught!"

As soon as the chest is full of rocks, the two men carry it back to where it was hidden, deep inside the cave. "Feels heavier than ever!" says Cap'n Binnacle. "When those rascals come to pick it up they're bound to think it's still full of gold!" "Splendid!" smiles Captain Cutlass. "I just wish I could see their faces when they find out they've been tricked!" "Come on!" calls Bill. "The pirates are on their way. I heard them singing a shanty as they set out towards the shore!"

Telling everyone to jump aboard, Cap'n Binnacle starts rowing as fast as he can. "It's as well I know the coastline!" he murmurs. "There are treacherous rocks lurking under these waters!" Keeping well out of sight, they round a headland and hurry back to Rocky Bay. "There are the pirates!" calls Rupert. "They're heading for the beach at Silversand . . ." "Well done!" gasps Cutlass as they land by the steps to Cap'n Binnacle's cabin. "That was a close run thing!"

RUPERT BEATS THE PIRATES

The Cap'n gives the chums a sack.
"We'll count the treasure in my shack . . ."

"The gold must be declared, but you
Can keep some as your rightful due!"

The chums bid their new friend farewell.
"I owe you more than words can tell!"

"There goes the **Gold Doubloon**! We taught
Her crew a lesson, lads! Well fought!"

Loading the treasure into sacks, Cap'n Binnacle leads the way up to his cabin. "Tip it out on this table!" he says. "We'll take a last look before we decide what to do . . ." "I suppose the Excise men will want it all back," sighs Captain Cutlass as the gold and jewels glimmer in the lamplight. "Perhaps not *all*!" smiles Cap'n Binnacle. "If you promise to give up piracy, you can keep a share to start a new life! The rest can go to the museum at Rocky Bay . . ."

"Time you lads were getting back!" says Cap'n Binnacle. "I'll show you the best way to go . . ." "Goodbye!" says Captain Cutlass. "Thank you for everything! If it hadn't been for you, I'd still be at the mercy of those mutinous marauders!" As they set out along the clifftop path Rupert spots a ship on the horizon, heading out to sea. "The *Gold Doubloon*!" he calls. "Good riddance!" says Cap'n Binnacle. "By the time they find the treasure's gone, they'll be half way round the Azores . . ."

RUPERT AND BILL WIN A PRIZE

Next time the two pals spot their friend
Their stay is nearly at an end . . .

The pirate captain's quit the sea –
"These old clothes are no use to me!"

In no time both the pals have made
Fine costumes for the grand parade . . .

"First prize!" the judge declares. "We feel
Your outfits look as though they're real!"

Later that week, Rupert and Bill are on their way back from the beach when they spot a familiar figure. "It's Cap'n Binnacle!" calls Rupert. "But who is that with him?" As the pair draw near, Rupert is astonished to see Captain Cutlass, who has clearly given up a life of piracy for ever . . . "Hello!" he smiles. "I thought you two might want these old clothes of mine for the Pirate Pageant. "How kind!" says Mrs. Bear. "I'm sure they'll look splendid!"

On the day of the Rocky Bay Pageant, Rupert and Bill dress up in their new costumes, then join the procession through the streets of the town. Captain Cutlass' jacket makes a marvellous coat for Rupert, while Bill wears his boots and a colourful waistcoat . . . At the end of the parade, the judges all decide to give the pair first prize. "Bravo!" cheers Cap'n Binnacle. "You'd almost think those two were real pirates!"

These two pictures look identical, but there are ten differences between them. Can you spot them all? *Answers on page 109.*

Who am I?

My first is in Bill (at the start, not the end),

My second's in Ottoline – Rupert's new friend.

My third rounds off Algy,

My fourth starts Bo-Peep, – the girl Rupert helps to search for her lost sheep.

My fifth starts Li-Poo, he's a wise Mandarin.

Uncle Polar's the name that my sixth letter's in.

My last begins Edward,

Now join in the game –

Put a letter in each box

And find out my name . . .

1	2	3

4	5	6	7

Paint a Picture

Can you paint a picture to go in this frame? It could be one of Ottoline's ancestors, a picture of Rupert or any of the other Nutwood chums . . .

Rupert's Crossword Puzzle

See if you can complete this crossword. All the answers can be found in stories from this year's annual . . .

ACROSS:
1. Hidden beach near Rocky Bay (10)
4. Rupert's best friend (4, 5)
5. Pong-Ping buys a box of these (7)
9. Hidden in a cave (8)
11. Scaly, fire-breathing creature (6)
13. Captain Cutlass' crew (7)
14. Brother of Freddy Fox (5)
15. Rupert's floats like a boat (3)
17. Rupert's chum from Nutwood Manor (8)
19. Rupert's pal – a pug (4)
20. King Frost's special powder (7)
21. Ruler of the sea (7)

DOWN:
1. Bringer of Christmas presents (5)
2. Sleepy island (3)
3. Wise inventor (9)
5. Pong-Ping's homeland (5)
6. Rupert's village (7)
7. Delivered by 16 down (7)
8. Lost by Bo-Peep (5)
10. Belongs to a baby (6)
12. Name of Captain Cutlass' ship (4, 8)
14. One in Nutwood freezes (8)
16. Shares railway carriage with Rupert and Mrs. Bear (7)
18. Celebrated by inhabitants of 5 down (3, 4)

Who has found the treasure?

What does it say?

Rupert and Bill have found a secret message in a bottle. "What does it say!" blinks Bill. "It's in code!" says Rupert. "Each number must stand for a letter. I wonder what happens if we try A=1, B=2 and so on until Z=26?" "Let's try!" says Bill. "The first number's 7 . . . that must be G!"

Answer on page 109.

Whose Hat?

Each of the hats shown above belongs to a character you have met in this year's Rupert Annual.
Can you work out who owns each one?

Answers on page 109.

Redirected Post

No wonder the postmen couldn't deliver these letters! Can you work out who they are for? *Answers on page 109.*

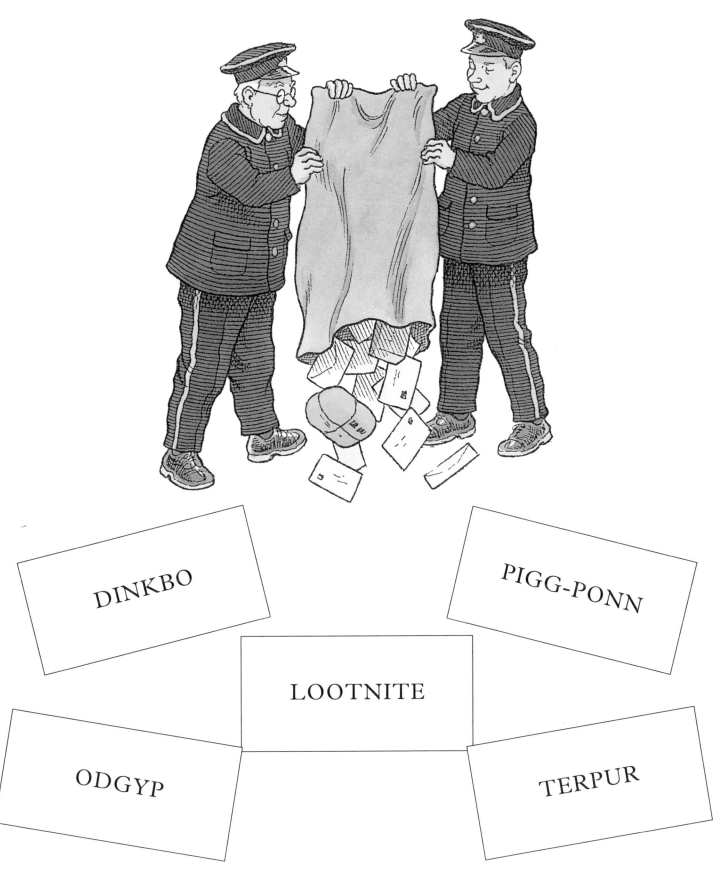

DINKBO

PIGG-PONN

LOOTNITE

ODGYP

TERPUR

How carefully can you colour these two pictures?

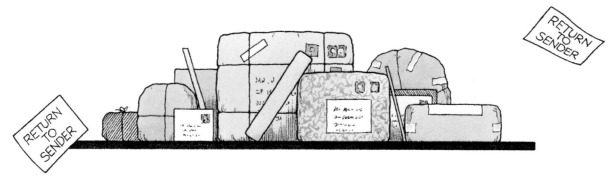

RUPERT
and the
Mail Train

RUPERT'S MOTHER PLANS A TRIP

Rupert goes shopping with his Mum.
The pair wait for their bus to come . . .

"To get to Nutchester we'll need
To catch a train next – the High Speed!"

"The train's just leaving! We're too late!
I don't suppose they'll make it wait . . ."

"Don't worry! There's another train . . ."
The Clerk says when the pair explain.

One autumn morning Rupert and his mother decide to go into Nutchester to visit the shops. "We'll make an early start," says Mrs. Bear. "I want to be there before it gets too crowded . . ." Rupert enjoys going on his mother's shopping expeditions as they normally travel to Nutchester by train. "Here's the bus for the station!" he calls excitedly. As they drive off, Mrs. Bear looks up the times of Nutchester trains. "That's good!" she says. "The next one's almost due."

When they arrive at the station, Rupert and his mother are dismayed to see that the train is already leaving. "We haven't even got tickets yet!" says Mrs. Bear. "I suppose we'll just have to catch the next one . . ." "Nutchester?" says the ticket clerk. "No need to worry! There should be another train along in a few minutes time. The one you missed was running late. I'll give you your tickets and you can wait on the platform until it comes. Nutchester will be the first stop."

RUPERT CATCHES A TRAIN

Soon, as they wait, the travellers see
A train approaching rapidly . . .

"Climb in!" says Mrs. Bear. "There's two
Free seats together that will do."

The other passenger inside
Their carriage sleeps throughout the ride.

Then Mrs. Bear gasps in dismay.
"We're travelling a different way!"

Sure enough, Rupert soon spots a train approaching the station. "This must be the one!" says Mrs. Bear. "We'll wait for it to stop, then look for an empty carriage . . ." To their surprise, the train is already quite crowded. "That's odd!" says Rupert's mother. "Perhaps it's Market Day? People must have travelled in from outlying villages." "I hope there are enough seats left for us!" says Rupert. "Yes," smiles Mrs. Bear. "Here are two together. Let's climb in . . ."

The only other passenger in the Bears' carriage is a postman, who is sound asleep. "He probably had an early start," says Rupert's mother. "In Nutwood, the post arrives before we've even finished breakfast!" Rupert gazes happily at the scenery as the train speeds along. Suddenly, the carriage gives a lurch and veers off along another line. "Oh dear!" says Mrs. Bear. "I'm sure this can't be right. *That* looks like the way to Nutchester, so where can we be going?"

RUPERT SEES THE POSTMEN ARRIVE

The postman wakes – amazed to see
He suddenly has company . . .

"This train's not meant for folk like you!
It only stops at our H.Q.!"

The train speeds on till Rupert sees
A building peeping through the trees.

"All change!" a voice begins to shout
As groups of postmen clamber out.

As Mrs. Bear peers anxiously out of the window the sleeping postman wakes with a start. "Hello!" he yawns. "Must have nodded off! Have we reached Nutwood yet?" "Yes," says Rupert. "That's where *we* got on . . ." "Intending to go to Nutchester," explains Mrs. Bear. "Dear me!" smiles the postman. "I'm afraid you're heading the wrong way! This is the Mail Train, you see. It only stops at Postal Headquarters after Nutwood. We're on a special branch line . . ."

The train speeds on, then finally slows to a halt. All Rupert can see is a large building, like some sort of castle . . . "Postal Headquarters!" calls a voice. "All change!" Stepping on to the platform, Rupert and his mother find themselves completely surrounded by postmen. Some start unloading sacks of mail, while others wheel bright red bicycles across the station yard. "Goodness!" blinks Mrs. Bear. "I'd no idea our letters came here! I wonder when the train goes back?"

RUPERT JOINS THE OTHERS

The friendly postman says he'll show
The visitors the way to go . . .

"The Postmaster can tell you when
The Nutwood train sets out again."

Rupert knocks at a bright red door.
"Come in!" a voice calls. "Join the tour!"

"Follow the others, please. This way!
We'll start off now, without delay . . ."

In the bustle of the crowd, Rupert spots the friendly postman, who shared their carriage. "I'm not sure about trains back to Nutwood," he says. "The best place to ask is at Head Office. Come with me and I'll show you where it is . . ." Leading the way to the large building Rupert saw earlier, the postman points towards a red door. "Ask for the Postmaster," he calls. "He'll sort something out. I'd come with you, if I wasn't on duty, but I'm afraid I have to go and join the sorting . . ."

Rupert knocks at the red door. "Come in!" calls a loud voice. Inside, a group of young postmen are being shown a plan of the building by the Postmaster . . . "This is where training starts," he declares. "Arrivals and Sorting. Join the others please. The tour's about to leave!" Before Mrs. Bear can say anything, everyone jumps to their feet and starts marching to the door. "Bit small for a postman!" declares the old man, looking at Rupert. "Still, we'll give him a chance . . ."

RUPERT SEES THE SORTING OFFICE

*"The sacks you see are full of post
That has been sent from coast to coast!"*

*"It all needs sorting out, you see,
Then sent on for delivery . . ."*

*"Remarkable!" blinks Mrs. Bear
As postmen hurry everywhere.*

*Next moment, Rupert catches sight
Of huge airships and planes in flight . . .*

Striding out of the room, the Postmaster leads Rupert and his mother along a corridor to join the other recruits. "Main Reception!" he cries. "This is where all the post arrives and is sent down to Sorting. Four deliveries a day. Comes from all over the World!" By this time, Rupert and Mrs. Bear are too fascinated to interrupt and follow the tour downstairs . . . "Sorting Office!" says their guide. "Letters, parcels, airmail. All filed by destination, then sent on their way."

As they follow the tour of Postal Headquarters, Rupert and his mother are astonished to see how letters and parcels are sent speeding along. "All at the double!" declares the Postmaster. "The faster, the better!" Marching briskly forward, he climbs a flight of steps and tells the new recruits to follow closely. Rupert is just about to join them, when he sees an open doorway, with blue sky beyond. "Airmail!" explains a postman. "Flights are leaving all day long. It's a wonderful sight . . ."

RUPERT SLIDES DOWN A CHUTE

The Postmaster explains that they
Have flights arrive and leave all day.

"I'll climb up for a better view!"
Thinks Rupert. "Then I'll see them too . . ."

But, suddenly, he feels the wall
Behind him move and starts to fall!

"Help!" Rupert cries. "I can't get out!"
But nobody can hear him shout . . .

Hurrying after the others, Rupert finds himself in a busy control tower, looking out over an airfield. "We can keep track of everything that comes and goes from up here!" declares the Postmaster proudly. "Outward post gets Top Priority." Rupert is fascinated by the special airships and clambers on to a nearby ledge to get a better view. "Runs like clockwork!" the Postmaster says. "Pilots know exactly where they're going and *we* know exactly where they are . . ."

Marvelling at the airships, Rupert hears the Postmaster tell the new recruits how many flights they make each day. Suddenly, he feels the wall behind him starting to move. "Help!" he gasps, losing his balance . . . Before anyone can move, Rupert tumbles head over heels down a smooth, steep chute, which seems to go on forever! As the door above closes, he is plunged into darkness, not knowing which way is up or down. "Oh, no!" he groans. "I hope I reach the bottom soon!"

RUPERT IS REDIRECTED

*He lands, at last, with such a bump
He makes a nearby postman jump.*

*"What's this? No label! I don't know!
No-one can tell where it should go!"*

*"Help!" Rupert calls out. "Stop the belt!"
But on it trundles, at full pelt.*

*He topples off the belt at last
And waits for someone to come past.*

At last Rupert spots a glimmer of light at the end of the chute. He lands with a bump in a huge jumble of parcels . . . "Bless me!" cries a startled postman. "This one's not even wrapped! No paper, no string and no sign of any address!" Poor Rupert is too shocked to speak as he's lifted clear of the parcels and put on a conveyor belt marked, "Redirected Mail". "They'll know what to do with it!" shrugs the postman. "I suppose the original label must have fallen off . . ."

The conveyor belt carries Rupert forward, past sacks of sorted mail. He tries calling for help but everyone is too busy to notice . . . "I don't suppose they can hear above the clatter!" he sighs. "It's going too fast to jump off, so I suppose I'd better just stay here and see what happens next!" The ride ends quite suddenly, with all the redirected post being tipped into a large basket. "Thank goodness!" thinks Rupert. "As soon as someone comes I'll tell them what's happened . . ."

RUPERT EXPLAINS AT LAST

But then the basket starts to sway
And Rupert finds he's wheeled away!

Another postman lifts him clear.
"Well, well!" he murmurs. "What's this here?"

"I'm not a parcel!" Rupert cries.
The postman blinks in stunned surprise . . .

As Rupert tells the way he fell
The Postmaster arrives as well.

Just as Rupert sits up, the basket full of redirected post begins to move . . . "Wait!" he calls as a postman tows it away. "I'm not a parcel!" To his dismay, the postman doesn't even look round, but simply leaves the basket and hurries on his way. "*He* didn't hear me either!" groans Rupert. At that moment a new postman starts to sort through the basket of post. "A walking bear!" he smiles as Rupert struggles to get free. "Fancy sending it through the post without a label . . ."

Lifting Rupert on to a workbench, the postman reaches for a sticky label marked, "Return to Sender". "You don't have to redirect me!" cries Rupert. "I've never been posted to start with!" "Not posted?" blinks the postman. "Then why were you in my basket?" "All an unfortunate accident!" booms the Postmaster as he strides towards the bench. "You led us quite a chase there, young man! Nearly ended up being delivered to your own house! No harm done, I'm glad to see!"

RUPERT HAS AN IDEA

*"Thank goodness!" Mrs. Bear cries. "We
Had no idea where you could be!"*

*"Trains back to Nutwood leave . . . oh, dear!
You've missed the last train back from here!"*

*"The airships that we saw! Do they
Pass over Nutwood on the way?"*

*"They might! Let's go and ask the crew
Exactly where they're flying to . . ."*

"Thank goodness you're safe!" cries Mrs. Bear. "I was worried when you suddenly disappeared!" "Sorry!" says Rupert. "At least I saw the Sorting Office . . ." "Your mother told me how you came to be here!" says the Postmaster. "It shouldn't be too difficult to get home. All you have to do, is catch the next train to Nutwood . . ." Unfolding a timetable, he reads through a list of destinations, then shakes his head in disbelief. "Can't be done!" he blinks. "The last train has already left!"

How can Rupert and his mother get back from Postal Headquarters now that they've missed the train? Thinking hard for a moment, he suddenly remembers all the airships he saw and asks the Postmaster if any of them ever fly over Nutwood. "Good idea!" says the old man. "We don't normally take passengers but this is an emergency! The last flights of the day should still be loading up. If we look lively we'll be able to see where they're going . . ."

RUPERT TAKES OFF

"Please keep the final airship moored.
Two passengers to come aboard!"

The pilot soon agrees to wait.
"But not for long or we'll be late!"

"Farewell! I hope you and your son
Enjoy the flight. It should be fun!"

The airship takes off silently
Then gathers speed quite rapidly . . .

Hurrying out to the courtyard, Rupert is dismayed to see that most of the airships have already left. "Wait!" calls the Postmaster. "Special consignment to go on the last flight!" The postman in charge leads them to a large balloon that is still being loaded with sacks of mail. "Just in time!" he cries. "A moment later and they'd have left too. It's a long distance flight, to Greenland and the North Pole . . ." Waving to the pilot, tells the others to follow him straightaway.

When they reach the airship, the pilot agrees to make a special detour over Nutwood. "Thank you for sorting everything out!" Rupert's mother tells the Postmaster. "I don't know *what* we'd have done without you . . ." "Don't mention it,!" he smiles. "Always glad to be of service." Without further ado, the huge airship rises into the sky, with Rupert peering excitedly through the cabin window. The propeller starts and they glide off, away from Postal Headquarters, across the open fields . . .

RUPERT FLIES HOME

"Look!" Mrs. Bear calls. "Down below!
There's somewhere there I think I know . . ."

"It must be Nutwood!" Rupert cries.
"Yes! Buildings that I recognise!"

"Because we're on a non-stop route
I'd like you both to parachute . . ."

"It's very safe. Jump when you see
Exactly where you'd like to be."

"This is wonderful!" gasps Mrs. Bear. "We're gliding along with hardly a sound . . ." Down below, Rupert can see fields and hedges, spread out like a giant map with model trees and houses. "You were lucky to catch us!" says the pilot. "Our timetable doesn't leave much room for extra stops. We normally fly north of Nutwood then out to sea. Makes a nice change to see a bit of countryside . . ." "Look!" cries Rupert. "There's Nutwood now! I can recognise the church tower."

As the airship hovers over Nutwood, the co-pilot asks Rupert and Mrs. Bear to come into the hold. "There isn't time for us to land," he explains. "You'll have to make a parachute jump . . ." "Super!" cries Rupert. "Are you sure it's safe?" asks his mother. "Absolutely!" smiles the pilot. "Strap these on and I'll show you what to do." When the pair are ready, he opens a hatch and points to the village below. "When you see your house, just jump out and the parachutes will open."

RUPERT AMAZES HIS FATHER

"There's our house now!" calls Mrs. Bear.
She jumps and floats down through the air.

As Rupert follows her he peers
Down at the road. "There's Dad!" he cheers.

"Great Scott!" he blinks as they drift down.
"I thought you'd both gone into town!"

"Don't tell me you flew there by plane?"
"No!" Rupert laughs. "We caught a train!"

"There's our house!" calls Mrs. Bear. "I suppose we'd better jump . . ." Rupert follows her out of the hatch and finds himself drifting gently down as the parachute billows out above his head. "How extraordinary!" gasps Mrs. Bear. "I'm flying over Nutwood like a bird!" "Wonderful!" calls Rupert. "We're going to land right in the front garden!" As they drift lower, he lets out a whoop of surprise. "There's Daddy!" he cries. "I can see him walking home along the path!"

Mr. Bear can hardly believe his eyes. "Hello!" calls Rupert. "We saw you as we were coming down!" "Coming down?" blinks his father. "Where from? Why are you both wearing parachutes?" "Nothing to worry about, dear!" laughs Mrs. Bear. "Rupert and I went on a journey to Nutchester . . ." "By aeroplane?" blinks Mr. Bear. "By train!" laughs Rupert. "We only came *back* by plane! Come inside and I'll tell you all about it . . ."

RUPERT and

*One morning, Rupert wakes to find
Ice patterns Jack Frost's left behind . . .*

One winter morning, Rupert wakes up to find icy patterns all over his bedroom window . . . "Jack Frost must have been here!" he laughs. "He draws on everyone's windows when winter starts!" The patterns are so pretty that Rupert calls for his mother to come and see. "How lovely!" she smiles. "The sun makes them sparkle like diamonds!" Rupert wonders if Jack is still in Nutwood. "Perhaps he'd let *me* draw patterns too?"

90

the Deep Freeze

"How beautiful!" smiles Mrs. Bear.
"They must mean Winter's in the air!"

"I'll look for Jack! Perhaps he'll know
When Nutwood's due to have some snow . . ."

As soon as he has finished breakfast, Rupert puts on his scarf and hurries outside. It is a crisp, sunny morning but very cold . . . "We must be due for snow soon!" he thinks. "I wonder if Jack knows when?" There is no sign of anyone in the village, so Rupert decides to look for his friend on Nutwood common. Jack Frost normally stays out of sight as he goes about his business but Rupert finally spots him, standing all alone . . .

"There's Jack Frost now! But what's he found?
It looks like something on the ground . . ."

RUPERT MEETS JACK FROST

*Then Rupert realises he
Has lost something. "What can it be?"*

*"My ice thermometer!" says Jack.
"For freezing things! I need it back!"*

*"I'll help you search," says Rupert. "For
It must be **somewhere** here – I'm sure!"*

*No matter how hard Rupert tries
He finds no sign. "It's gone!" he sighs.*

To Rupert's surprise, Jack Frost seems to be searching for something. "Hello!" he calls and hurries to join him. "Who's there?" says Jack. "Oh, Rupert! I was so busy I didn't hear you coming . . ." "What have you lost?" asks Rupert. "My thermometer!" sighs Jack. "I'll be in trouble unless I find it!" "We've got one," says Rupert. "Not like mine," says Jack. "It freezes everything it touches. I use it to draw on window panes. My father gave it to me as a special present!"

Rupert offers to help search for the missing thermometer. "It looks like an icicle," Jack tells him. "Be careful not to touch the tip, or else it will freeze you too!" The pair split up, with Rupert combing the common while Jack covers the rest of Nutwood . . . "I can't see any icicle!" thinks Rupert. "Perhaps it's fallen into one of these bushes or got buried in a clump of grass?" The longer Rupert searches, the harder it seems. "Like looking for a needle in a haystack!" he sighs.

RUPERT FINDS A FROZEN POND

Then someone calls out Rupert's name.
"Hey! Come and join our sliding game!"

"A frozen pond!" he blinks. "What fun!
It's big enough for everyone . . ."

The pals walk home and Rupert sees
The fountain's not begun to freeze . . .

His parents think it's strange the way
That only one pond froze today . . .

Rupert is still looking for Jack Frost's thermometer when he hears the sound of laughter. "It's Podgy and the others!" he smiles. "They're sliding on a frozen pond!" Hurrying to join his chums, he hears how the Fox brothers found the pond and couldn't resist trying it out. "Why don't *you* have a go?" calls Freddy. "The ice is so thick, it's quite safe!" Rupert takes a run up, then goes whizzing after the others. "Hurrah!" he cries as they slither and slide, over and over again . . .

At last the chums have had enough of their game and everyone makes their way back to Nutwood. "It's odd that nothing else is frozen!" thinks Rupert. "The village fountain normally stops as soon as the weather turns icy but it's flowing as fast as ever . . ." Rupert's parents are surprised to hear about the frozen pond as well. "How odd!" says Mrs. Bear. "Perhaps a freak wind chilled the pond!" "That must be it!" nods Rupert's father. "The barometer said we'd have sunshine . . ."

RUPERT IS MYSTIFIED

*Next morning, Mr. Bear finds more
Ice patterns – different from before . . .*

*"A funny drawing!" Rupert blinks.
"That can't be Jack Frost's work!" he thinks.*

*His mother gives a startled cry.
"My washing's like a board!" But why?*

*"It must have frozen in the night."
"My word!" gasps Mr. Bear, "you're right!"*

Next morning, Rupert comes downstairs to find a new set of icy patterns on the window panes. "They look different today!" says Mr. Bear. "The ones in the kitchen were more like scribble than pretty flowers . . ." Peering outside, he gives a gasp of surprise, then calls Rupert over to see. "I don't believe it!" he tuts. "It must be one of your chums!" Rupert peers at the drawing. "That doesn't look like one of Jack Frost's drawings!" he says. "But who else could have made it?"

When breakfast is over, Rupert and his parents find more surprises out in the garden . . . "Come and look at my washing!" cries Mrs. Bear. "It's frozen stiff!" "Impossible!" says Rupert's father. "The lawn isn't even white . . ." Unpegging a shirt from the line, he holds it up, then shakes his head in disbelief. "Are you sure you didn't use too much starch?" he blinks. "No!" says Mrs. Bear. "It's all cold and icy. We must have had a sudden frost overnight."

RUPERT SLIPS ON THE ICE

The High Street's frozen too, it seems.
The icy pavement glints and gleams . . .

"Help!" Rupert cries. He stops his fall
By clutching at a nearby wall!

A lorry's slipped as well. Its load
Is scattered all across the road!

Then Rupert stops, amazed at how
The village fountain's frozen now . . .

Leaving his parents to puzzle over the frozen washing, Rupert sets off towards the High Street in search of his chums. He hasn't gone far, when he sees a crowd of people gathered together by the side of the road. Hurrying towards them, he finds the pavement is covered in a fine layer of slippery ice. "There must have been a frost after all!" he gasps. "I wonder why it seems so patchy?" Clutching the top of the wall, he sets off again, to see why everyone is staring . . .

When Rupert reaches the High Street, the crowd is so large that he has to push forward to see what is causing the commotion. A lorry has skidded on a patch of ice and shed its load! Parcels and packages lie in a jumbled heap as P.C. Growler tries to clear the way. "It's lucky no-one was hurt!" says Mrs. Badger. "Yes!" nods the Professor. "I'm amazed everywhere's so icy! Just look at the village fountain . . ." To Rupert's astonishment, it is completely covered in ice!

RUPERT SOLVES THE MYSTERY

The Fox twins shuffle past the throng.
A bandaged Ferdy limps along . . .

"The fountain froze so fast he fell
And dropped the magic wand as well!"

"Wand?" Rupert asks. The twins admit
They drew on window panes with it . . .

There, in the fountain, Rupert sees
Jack's missing wand that makes things freeze!

Rupert is still marvelling at the fountain when he spots the Fox brothers coming out of Dr. Lion's surgery. Poor Ferdy has his foot bandaged up and is hobbling along with a stick. "What's happened?" asks Rupert. "Did you slip on the ice?" "That's right," says Freddy. "It froze so quickly we were taken by surprise." "Goodness!" blinks Rupert. "I've never heard of ice freezing *that* fast before. Where did you fall?" "From the fountain!" says Ferdy. "I slid off and dropped the magic wand!"

"Magic wand?" asks Rupert. "Yes," says Ferdy. "We found it up on the common . . ." "Jack Frost's thermometer!" Rupert cries. "He uses it to draw patterns on everyone's windows." "*We* tried that!" admits Freddy. "Then we found we could freeze things as well!" Leading Rupert to the fountain's edge, he points down at a glowing light. "*That's* what's making everything icy!" he explains. "The water froze so quickly we couldn't get it back. Now the ice is spreading, all over Nutwood!"

RUPERT TELLS THE PROFESSOR

"Hello!" the old Professor cries.
"This ice is rather a surprise!"

*Rupert explains he knows what's made
The ice. "It's trapped here, I'm afraid!"*

*The Professor tells Bodkin they
Will need a blow-lamp straightaway . . .*

*"We need to melt the ice before
This magic wand makes any more!"*

As Rupert and Freddy peer down into the ice, they are joined by the Professor, who has come to take a closer look at the fountain. "Fascinating!" he declares. "Everything seems to have frozen so fast!" "Perhaps!" gulps Freddy. "Can't think why! I'd better be off now, Rupert. Got to help Ferdy get home . . ." Without mentioning the Foxes, Rupert tells the Professor how Jack Frost's thermometer is frozen inside the fountain. "That's why Nutwood has suddenly grown so cold!"

While most people would be astonished by Rupert's story, the Professor simply nods his head. "Of course! If the thermometer makes things cold, then ice will go on forming until it's taken out of the fountain . . ." He thinks for a moment, then sends Bodkin to his workshop to fetch a blow-lamp. "Thawing the ice is our only hope," he explains as his servant comes hurrying back. "Chipping it away would take far too long. If something's not done soon, the whole village will be iced-up . . ."

The blow-lamp starts to thaw the ice.
"We'll have the wand free in a trice!"

To everyone's dismay they see
The ice re-forming instantly!

Next morning ice is everywhere.
"It's freezing cold!" says Mrs. Bear.

The fountain's disappeared from sight
Beneath an icy mound of white . . .

Bodkin points the blow-lamp at the frozen fountain. "It's melting!" smiles Rupert. "The moment he's finished, I'll reach in and grab Jack's thermometer . . ." Soon Bodkin pushes back his goggles and turns off the lamp. "That's better!" he declares, but, to Rupert's dismay, the water freezes over. "Try again!" orders the Professor, but it's no use. Each time the ice melts, it freezes straightaway. "What a dilemma!" he sighs. "We'll have to think of something else . . ."

Next morning, the ice from the fountain has spread so far it covers the whole village . . ."You'll need to wrap up warm!" says Mrs. Bear as she hands Rupert his coat. "Be careful not to slip, dear. The path looks like a skating rink!" As he sets off along the High Street, there are icicles hanging from every window and the fountain has vanished under a frozen mound."The Professor's here already!" he smiles as he spots his old friend, standing by the fountain, lost in thought . . .

RUPERT FLIES NORTH

The old Professor can't think how
To stop the ice from spreading now . . .

At last the friends agree to go
And visit Jack Frost. "He might know!"

"We're flying North, across the sea.
Rupert can navigate for me . . ."

The pair take off and quickly find
They've left the English coast behind . . .

The Professor stares at the fountain and shakes his head. "It's no use!" he declares. "Each time we melt the ice it's sure to freeze again . . ." "Jack Frost's thermometer's causing the trouble!" says Rupert. "If we told *him* what's happened, he might know how to stop it!" "Good idea!" nods the Professor. "He lives at the North Pole, doesn't he?" "That's right," says Rupert. "His father has a palace made of ice." "Come on!" says the Professor. "We'll fly there, straightaway . . ."

As soon as the pair reach the Professor's tower, he leads the way to his latest aircraft. "There's only room for two of us," he tells Bodkin. "You stay here, while Rupert helps me navigate." The little servant fills the plane's fuel tank and helps Rupert clamber into the cockpit. The Professor starts the engine and soon they are soaring high over Nutwood, off towards the coast. "I'll keep flying North towards the Pole!" calls the Professor. "Tell me when you spot the palace . . ."

RUPERT ENCOUNTERS A SNOWSTORM

Icebergs and jagged peaks appear.
"The North Pole must be getting near . . ."

A sudden snowstorm starts to blow –
The pair can't see which way to go!

"Who knows how long this storm might last?
We'll have to land until it's passed . . ."

"We'll wait until the snow stops then
I'll try to find the Pole again!"

For a long time all that Rupert can see is the blue of the ocean down below. At last he spots the jagged peaks of distant mountains and massive icebergs. "This is the start of the Polar ice!" says the Professor. "We shouldn't have much further to go . . ." As he speaks, a dark cloud looms on the horizon, growing larger and larger, until it fills the whole sky. "A snowstorm!" gasps Rupert as icy winds buffet the little plane. "We'll have to land!" calls the Professor. "I can't see where I'm going!"

By the time the little plane lands it is completely covered in a thick layer of snow. "This is terrible!" groans the Professor. "The blizzard has blown us off course and I can't tell where we are . . ." Unfolding a map, he shows Rupert the path they were taking and the spot where the Pole should be. "We'll just have to wait till it stops snowing!" he declares. "If we leave the plane now we're bound to get lost. When the blizzard's over I'll use my compass to find the way."

RUPERT MEETS UNCLE POLAR

Then, suddenly, a polar bear
Surprises the astonished pair!

It's Rupert's Uncle Polar, who
Lives nearby, in a large igloo . . .

"Come in!" he smiles delightedly.
"You've just dropped by in time for tea!"

Polar agrees to guide the friends.
"We'll set off when this blizzard ends . . ."

Suddenly, Rupert hears someone tapping at the window of the plane. "A wild polar bear!" gasps the Professor. "Uncle Polar!" cries Rupert. "*He's* not wild. He lives at the North Pole . . ." Rupert's uncle is delighted to see the visitors from Nutwood and invites them to come and shelter in his igloo. "The snowstorm should blow over in a while," he says. "Come and tell me what you're up to!" The Professor blinks in surprise as Polar leads the way across the snow towards his special house . . .

The Professor is even more surprised to see *inside* the igloo, for Polar's house is far bigger than it seems . . . "Come and have tea!" he says. "It's nice to have guests drop in. I don't get many visitors." When he hears how Nutwood has been covered in ice, Polar agrees that King Frost is the only person who can sort things out. "He lives in a great ice palace, quite near the Pole. I'll take you there when this blizzard stops. It's easy to find when you know the way . . ."

RUPERT SETS OUT

"Clear skies!" smiles Polar. "Time to go!
I'll lead the way across the snow!"

The Professor says he'll fly back
While Rupert goes to visit Jack.

"Jack's father's palace lies nearby
The Northern Lights. Just watch the sky . . ."

"It's like a rainbow!" Rupert blinks.
"And that must be Jack's home!" he thinks.

When everyone has finished tea, Uncle Polar steps outside to see if the blizzard is over. "Clear skies!" he calls. "We won't be troubled again . . ." As Polar knows King Frost, he offers to take Rupert to the ice palace while the Professor flies back to Nutwood. "Good idea!" smiles the Professor. "I'll tell your parents you're in safe hands. If you need any help, just give me a call!" Climbing back into the plane, he starts the engine and is soon soaring off, up into the sky . . .

Uncle Polar sets off towards King Frost's palace. "You'll know we're getting near when you spot the Northern Lights!" he says. "Keep watching until you see the sky change colour . . ." Rupert follows his uncle across the snowy wastes, amazed that he can find the way. "It's my home!" laughs Polar. "In Nutwood, *you'd* have to show *me* where to go!" After a while, the sky turns from blue to pink, then to a brilliant green. "Northern Lights!" smiles Polar. "And there's King Frost's palace . . ."

RUPERT ENTERS THE ICE PALACE

The pair approach a palace where
Two guards stand sentry. "Halt! Who's there?"

When Polar mentions King Frost's son
They say he can't see anyone . . .

"I'm sure King Frost will talk to me!
I'd like to see him urgently!"

At last the guard agrees to bring
The pair to see Jack and the King . . .

As they approach the glittering palace, Rupert sees two sentries guarding at the main gate. "Who's there?" they ask. "What business have you with King Frost?" "I've come to see his son," replies Rupert. "Jack and I have often met, during his winter visits to Nutwood . . ." "Young Master Jack is in disgrace for losing his thermometer!" declares the guard. "The King has forbidden him any visitors for the rest of the week. If you want to see him, you'll have to come back later . . ."

"Impossible!" cries Uncle Polar. "Rupert has come here on an urgent mission! Tell King Frost I *insist* on seeing him." The guard delivers Polar's message and soon comes back to announce that the King will receive them immediately. As he enters the throne room, Rupert spots Jack, still being scolded by his father." "Oh, dear!" he thinks. "I hope he won't be too cross when he hears what's happened. Supposing he decides it serves us right and leaves Nutwood to freeze all winter?"

RUPERT ASKS KING FROST TO HELP

The King hears how the wand Jack dropped
Will freeze Nutwood unless it's stopped . . .

"Fetch thawing powder straightaway –
We need to act without delay!"

In no time, Jack comes running back
And hands the King a little sack . . .

"Watch!" says King Frost. "This powder's sure
To make the thickest ice all thaw!"

Although King Frost looks cross, he nods to Uncle Polar and asks what brings his nephew all the way to the North Pole. When he hears how the lost thermometer has covered Nutwood in a layer of ice, he shakes his head and declares it is all a result of Jack's carelessness. "*You* caused the Freeze, so *you* shall help to end it!" he tells his son. "Fetch a sack of thawing powder from the cellar as quickly as you can. Tell the guards to make sure it's the strongest they can find . . ."

To Rupert's surprise, Jack returns with a small sack, hardly bigger than a bag of flour . . . "Well done!" says the King. "This should soon solve Nutwood's problems, but I'll test a little first, to make sure it works . . ." Taking a pinch of powder from the sack, he sprinkles it on the frozen window-sill. Almost at once, the ice begins to melt, vanishing before Rupert's astonished gaze. "Double strength!" says the King. "Thaws ice and snow in the blink of an eye!"

RUPERT LEAVES THE PALACE

Rupert and Polar thank the King.
His powder should solve everything . . .

They say goodbye to Jack Frost too.
"I'll send the wand straight back to you!"

Then Rupert asks his uncle how
He'll travel back to Nutwood now . . .

"Don't worry!" Polar smiles. "You'll see!
There's something you can take for me . . ."

"I *knew* you would be able to help!" says Polar as he takes the Thawing Powder from King Frost. "We polar bears enjoy ice and snow all year round, but down in Nutwood they don't like being too chilly!" Rupert tells Jack that he'll get his thermometer back for him as soon as the fountain melts. "I'm sure your father won't be cross for long! You didn't *mean* to freeze Nutwood. It was only an accident, after all!" "Come on!" says Uncle Polar. "It's time we were on our way . . ."

"How am I going to get to Nutwood?" asks Rupert as the pair walk back across the snow. "Will you telephone the Professor and ask him to collect me?" "Don't worry!" laughs Polar. "There's someone else who can take you, even faster than the Professor's plane. We've arranged to meet at my igloo, just after tea-time . . ." As they near Polar's house, Rupert can see no sign of a visitor. "Who is it?" he asks. "You'll see!" smiles his uncle.

Rupert tells Polar he can hear
The sound of sleigh bells drawing near . . .

"It's Santa Claus! He's in his sleigh –
Piled high with toys for Christmas Day!"

"Hello!" blinks Santa. "Rupert Bear
From Nutwood! I'm just going there!"

"You'd better fly back home with me!"
The pair take off immediately . . .

The moment they arrive at the igloo, Uncle Polar unlocks a cupboard and reaches inside. "There's a special package I want you to take . . ." he begins but breaks off as Rupert hears the sound of jingling bells. "Look outside!" chuckles Polar. When Rupert crawls out of the igloo he is astonished to see a reindeer-drawn sledge swooping down from the sky. "Santa Claus!" he gasps. "Of course! It's Christmas Eve. He must be on his way to deliver all the children's presents . . ."

Santa is astonished to see Rupert at the North Pole. "I thought you'd be in Nutwood!" he says. "I'm just on my way there to deliver all your presents." "That's why Santa's come visiting!" laughs Polar. "He was going to take a present from me as well . . ." When he hears how Rupert plans to save Nutwood from being buried in ice, Santa agrees to take him there on his sledge. "You're lucky it's the next place on my list," he says. "I hope we won't find it's too icy to land . . ."

106

RUPERT RETURNS TO NUTWOOD

The sky grows dark and stars come out.
"There won't be anyone about . . ."

They spot the village, down below,
"It looks as if it's thick with snow!"

"The fountain!" Rupert calls. "I'll try
To sprinkle dust as we fly by . . ."

The ice all disappears and then
The fountain starts to work again!

Darkness falls as Santa's reindeer speed on their way to Nutwood. Rupert explains how King Frost has given him a sack full of special powder to thaw the frozen village. "There it is now!" he calls excitedly. "I can see the church tower and everybody's houses . . ." "They should all be tucked up in bed by now," says Santa. "We'll fly over the rooftops and you can sprinkle your powder without being seen. It looks so white and frosty, you'd almost think it had been snowing!"

Santa's sleigh circles over the sleeping village, flying lower and lower, until Rupert spots Nutwood's frozen fountain. Carefully untying King Frost's sack of powder, he reaches over the side and sprinkles a generous handful on the huge mound of ice . . . "I'll land nearby, so we can see if there's any change," announces Santa. By the time the sleigh stops, Rupert is sure he can hear the sound of splashing water. "Look!" he gasps. "It's working! The fountain has thawed already . . ."

RUPERT RECOVERS JACK'S WAND

"I've got it!" Rupert cries. "Now Jack
Can have his thermometer back!"

"Well done! Give me the powder too.
I'll sprinkle all the rest for you!"

Next morning, Rupert wakes to find
A present Santa's left behind . . .

"Skates!" Rupert laughs. "Although they're nice
I think we've had enough of ice!"

Peering into the trough of the fountain, Rupert can see Jack Frost's thermometer, glowing at the bottom. Rolling up his sleeve, he reaches down and lifts it to the surface. "At last!" he cries. "To think it's caused all this trouble . . ." Santa tells Rupert that he will take the thermometer back to Jack when he returns to the North Pole. "I'll take the rest of your powder too," he adds. "I can sprinkle it over Nutwood as I put everyone's presents down the chimney pots."

Next morning, Rupert wakes to find the ice has already melted. At the foot of his bed is a colourful stocking full of presents. "There's the parcel Uncle Polar gave me!" he thinks and hurries to unwrap it straightaway. "Ice skates!" laugh his parents when they see what he has been given. "Normally, I'd wish for a snowy Christmas!" smiles Rupert, "But after all that's happened I don't mind waiting a little while before I try them out . . ."

Follow Rupert every day

John Harrold.

in the Daily Express

ANSWERS TO PUZZLES:

(P.68) Spot the Difference: 1) Present missing; 2) Toy soldier's hat missing; 3) Pencils missing from pot on chest of drawers; 4) Bookend missing; 5) Toy car missing; 6) Knob missing from chest of drawers; 7) Picture missing from wall; 8) Leg missing from bedside table; 9) Buttons missing from Rupert's pyjamas; 10) Slippers missing under bed.

(P.69) Who am I?: BOY BLUE

(P.71) Crossword:

Across	Down
1. Silversand	1. Santa
4. Bill Badger	2. Nod
5. Candles	3. Professor
9. Treasure	5. China
11. Dragon	6. Nutwood
13. Pirates	7. Letters
14. Ferdy	8. Sheep
15. Bed	10. Rattle
17. Ottoline	12. Gold Doubloon
19. Algy	14. Fountain
20. Thawing	16. Postman
21. Neptune	18. New Year

(P.73) What does it say?:
GREETINGS FROM ROCKY BAY

(P.74) Whose Hat?:
1) King Frost; 2) Li-Poo; 3) Chang; 4) Mrs. Bear; 5) The Professor; 6) Cap'n Binnacle; 7) Gaffer Jarge; 8) Ice Palace guard; 9) Captain Cutlass; 10) Santa; 11) Boy Blue; 12) The Piper; 13) The Postmaster; 14) Jack Frost; 15) Rupert – Chinese costume; 16) Bill – pirate costume.

(P.75) Redirected Post:
DINKBO = BODKIN
PIGG-PONN = PONG-PING
LOOTNITE = OTTOLINE
TERPUR = RUPERT
ODGYP = PODGY